SEEDS

The Journey Begins

Cary Allen Stone

Cary Allen Stone

Contents

Characters

Dr. Bryan Neumeister, Astrophysicist, Co-founder

Dr. Isaac Arthur, Astrophysicist, Co-founder

Dr. Alexandra "Alex" Arthur, Physicist

Dr. Rebecca Adkins, Asst. to Dr. Arthur

Dr. Elan Mason, Founder of SpaceTech

Dr. Trent Garth, World-Renowned Cosmologist

Dr. Michael Talbot, Astrophysicist, Project Manager

Dr. Clifford Baker, Chief Medical Officer

Dr. Ted Thurgood, Bioengineering

Dr. James Fulbright, Bioengineering, Neurosurgeon

Dr. Steven Winslow, Bioengineering

Dr. Robert Sanders, Robotics

Dr. Phillip Britte, Fabrication

Dr. Tom Patterson, GPS Systems

Dr. Peter Wiggins, Waste Control.

Dr. Seth Rogers, Flexible Composite Materials

Dr. Bob Hinkle, Space Communications & Navigation

Dr. Elliot Hammerstein, Laser Development

Dr. Phillip Clemons, Propulsion

Commander John Kelly

Captain Brenda Holder

Captain Hunter Ragsdale

First Officer Lukas Easton

First Officer Rhian Estefan

First Officer Sean McNeal

Systems Control & Navigation Edward Kingston

Systems Control & Navigation Officer Susan Wright

Systems Control & Navigation Officer Hank Stillwater

Weapons Control Specialist Danny Chan

Weapons Control Specialist Tommy Maxwell

Weapons Control Specialist Ricky Tinsdale

Weapons Control Specialist George TwoBears

Acronyms

SEEDS, Strategic Extra-Earth Development Site
DARPA, Defense Advanced Research Projects Agency
VASIMR, Variable Specific Impulse Magnetoplasma Rocket
ANNULAR, Ion Propulsion Thruster
SE-15, SpaceTech Engine Small & Large Nozzle
MHD, Magnetohydrodynamic
TC, Thruster Controls
MFC, Master Flight Computer
PFD, Primary Flight Display
HUD, Heads-Up Display
EPM, Engineering & Propulsion Maintenance
BCS, Backup Control Station
FRM, Fabricated Rocket Module
EFT, External Fuel Tank
LDC, Laser Directed Canon
LDA, Large Detector Array
RG, Rail Gun
VOE, Vault of Embryos
GR, Gravity Ring
VA, Virtual Autopsy
LMI, Laser Measurement Instrument
TCU, Targeting Control Unit
AGL, Above Ground Level
GPR, Ground Proximity Radar
DOI, Dangerous Organism Inspection

More by Cary Allen Stone:

SEEDS The Journey Begins
Science Fiction

The Jake Roberts Novels:
Crime Fiction

After the Evil
Book 1

Mind Over Murder
Book 2

After the Goode
Book 3

After The Kill
Book 4

After You're Dead
Book 5

Stealing Atlanta
Thriller

Through a Mother's Eyes
True Crime

For Tyler, Rocky,
Kelly, Kyle, Vinny,
Brian, Rachel, Julia, Baby, Toby

Foreword

SEEDS: The Journey Begins takes what we know today and adds what we think is coming tomorrow regarding technology, science, and colonization. The questions I wanted to answer are: If we listen to the warnings that humanity must leave the Earth in one hundred years to survive, what would a ship look like today, or the next few years? What kind of propulsion is available? What would it feel like to travel for an extended time to reach a moon in our own galaxy? Do we really want to go to Mars? What about deep space? What would a colony be like on a new world?

I want to thank Bryan Neumeister who also shares my passion for science, and is the most respected audio forensics technician in the U.S. and abroad.

I want to thank Isaac Arthur who kept my science straight. See him on YouTube at *Science & Futurism with Isaac Arthur.*

—CAS

SEEDS

The Journey Begins

CHAPTER 1

"Who were the gods of the Ancients?
Are we the gods now?"
—Michael Talbot, Astrophysicist

The board considered the probability of war, and decided to change course from Mars, to Saturn's moon, Titan. The excitement among the employees resembled a high-energy burst inside the particle separator at CERN.

Alex and Michael sat in the facilities cafeteria. They used their lunch breaks to exchange views as trusted confidants. He cut through the cod with his fork, and dipped it into the tartar sauce. He put his fork down, and opened a bottle of water.

"I hope these vegetables taste as good on Titan," she said.

Michael checked his watch, it was time to get back to work. Alex stood with her tray. Michael waited for her to pass. They delivered them to the carousel.

Dr. Michael Talbot was one of the first astrophysicists brought into the SEEDS program by Dr. Bryan Neumeister, and Dr. Isaac Arthur. On Talbot's office walls were degrees from MIT, Stanford, and Oxford next to a Nobel Prize. As

Project Manager, he had access to futuristic technology, and control over the construction of an intergalactic ship, and a space colony.

On Dr. Alexandra "Alex" Arthur's wall hung a PhD in physics from MIT. Her father, Dr. Isaac Arthur, had built the second most profitable tech empire.

The wealthiest man on Earth, Dr. Bryan Neumeister, was a tech giant who co-founded SEEDS, the Strategic Extra-Earth Development Site, with Arthur. The ultra-secure, space exploration development facility did super-science research, and created mind-freaking technology.

On a limited basis, SEEDS shared specific developments with DARPA, and NASA's Ames Research Center located across from the facility on Moffett Federal Field, a joint civilian/military airport northwest of San Jose.

Administration was on Level 1. The board kept a sharp eye out for anyone with a new technology, or skill set, which benefited SEEDS. Human Resources tracked the brightest university graduates and specialists in their disciplines who could contribute to the project.

Subterranean Levels 2 and 3 housed Bioengineering, Biology, and the Cryogenics Labs. Bioengineering worked with DNA to genetically alter humans to make them stronger giving them a better chance of surviving on a new world. The researchers were able to bypass the Darwinian evolutionary process. It would only take them months to do what nature did in centuries, or millennia. In an ultra-secure lab in Bioengineering, scientists did research in biohacking. They pushed the boundaries of ethical and legal norms. Inside, it was a brave new world. The Biology lab created storage and maintenance systems for the frozen embryos traveling on the flight. The embryos would be backup for the humans who failed to last the entire trip, and for newborn colonists once they reached their destination. They would also preserve every animal, and plant species. Some of those boarding the flight wanted to arrive on Titan frozen with no desire to observe the galaxy they would traverse. Cryogenics fitted them for cryo-beds. Inside the beds, the temperature would be reduced to 93° to slow body functions. Intravenous feeding would provide the nutrients the body needs, and tubes for human waste. When they awoke, they would be a billion-plus miles from Earth.

Fabrication, Robotics, Space Communications and Navigation occupied Level 4. The advances in robotics were miraculous. Humans had for decades altered their medical and mental sensory with augmentations which qualified them as Cyborgs. Robotics fine-tuned the process. Fabrication refined the 10-D printers, so they could construct any sized object adaptable to the natural resources of the moon. During the flight, they would manufacture parts required for ship repairs. Upon arrival on Titan, they would provide necessary structural components for the colony. Space Communications and Navigation designed navigation route maps, approach profiles, and interplanetary space buoys.

Hydroponics, Food and Water was on Level 5.

The hydroponic gardens and fish farms would be a central source of food. They developed a human waste recycling system that transferred human waste to the hydroponic bays to fertilize the plants. From the bays, the system piped to the fish farms. After the fish dined, the water was filtered, purified, and recycled in the reservoir. Between the inner and outer hulls for the entire length of the ship, the sleeve tanks would store freshwater from Earth. By saving the water this way, the travelers received an added benefit because the water was a natural insulation against dangerous radiation in space. The freshwater supply would last until sources of water on the planet could sustain the colony. Once the scientists discovered an underground lake or ocean, they would use in-situ resource production. Using the Sabatier reaction, the underground water and the carbon dioxide in the atmosphere would be synthesized to produce water. The researchers examined the food chain and decided which animals had the best chances of survival on the moon. They worked closely with Cryogenics to adapt animals into cryogenic stasis. They could save on the weight of feed for the animals, and add precious storage space.

The cockpit simulators on Level 6 were in constant use, either for training, or testing communications and navigation equipment. Programmed into the computers were every possible scenario the crew and passengers might encounter during the flight. The flight crews spent most of their time there, and when not in training were sent to the labs to learn about the latest developments.

Propulsion was on the deepest subterranean level, Level 7. They could control the sound of the propulsion systems they were testing with layers of soundproofing. They tried to keep the noise at an acceptable decibel, but when they ran the engines in synchronization, they set off seismic counters around the globe. Seismologists wrote each test off as the usual shifting of the tectonic plates on the West Coast. Oklahoma ran interference having been frakked causing more earthquakes than anywhere on the planet.

Neumeister, Arthur, and a chosen group of edgy scientists believed the logical solution to the traumas plaguing the planet was no longer to repair Mother Earth, but to leave her, and find a new home for humanity. They developed, viable solutions using current technology. Their central focus was on launching SEEDS–2025.

Bryan, Isaac, and Steven discussed the change to Titan.

"Today's news reports say tensions between nuclear armed countries is reaching critical mass. Intelligence reports say the Chinese and Russians are focused on colonizing Mars. We are fortunate to have selected Titan. We will avoid any conflict should it spill over to the colonies occupying territory on Mars," Bryan said.

"We not soldiers. We're scientists. We want to know more about the universe," Isaac said.

"I have a question," Dr. Winslow said.

"Yes, Doctor."

"How far can we step out of the box?"

"Both feet if you can create a useful new technology for the ship, colony, or colonists. We will provide what you need to build it, but make sure it's not some mad scientist nonsense."

It didn't take long for any of them to go outside the box because most had already ventured there. Bryan asked Becca to have Dr. Hammerstein come to his office. He entered, a towering man who kept to himself.

"Elliot, I want you to build a system powerful enough to take out a satellite, space station, or a hostile ship."

"Immediately, Dr. Neumeister."

"Are you free for the next hour?" Michael asked.

"I could be, why?" Alex said.

"I want you to see something."

He received a report of a significant breakthrough in Bioengineering. They rode the elevator to Level 3. Michael waited for the facial recognition scan. The heavy door opened, and he led Alex inside. They waited for a second door to open, which did with a hiss. The lab was sterile. In the next chamber, they put on lab coats and surgical masks. Dr. Ted Thurgood greeted them. They walked down hallway until they arrived at a hospital room on the left. Thurgood asked Alex to wait in the hall. He and Michael went inside. Across the hall was an array of computers and monitors in a control room. Michael saw neurosurgeon, Dr. James Fulbright, lean over the test subject. He had implanted a chip in the man's brain, which would allow him to access the entire recorded history and knowledge of mankind.

The implant illuminated several annunciators in the control room indicating it was operational. James prodded the patient to be responsive after sedation. Wires covered most of the area from the back of his skull to computers across the hall. His vitals looked good, but he was groggy. His eyelids fluttered like the wings of a butterfly. He managed a smile as James looked into each eye with a flashlight.

"Trent?"

His eyes opened.

"James."

The test subject was renowned cosmologist, Dr. Trent Garth.

It was a high-five moment for Fulbright's research team. Michael leaned in.

"How are you, Trent."

"Michael, I'm anxious to get on the ship. I look forward to observing the marvels of our galaxy, and Titan. A colony on Titan means we will reach outer space defined as the distance from Saturn, to the Kuiper Belt."

"You will advance our mission by light years after going through the surgery. What better place for the most powerful mind in the universe than to sail through it?"

On the ship, and in the colony, Trent would be invaluable for research, and guidance to the crew.

James leaned down.

"You have access to humankind's recorded knowledge, feel free to explore it. I'll be in the control room."

Michael walked into the hall.

"Is it true?" Alex asked.

"No one knows he's here, except those who work with James, Bryan, and your dad."

James stood next to Michael.

"The implant nested perfectly."

"Can I go in?" Alex asked.

"Yes, of course."

She never met him. To Alex and the community, Dr. Trent Garth, was a scientist's rock star.

"It's an honor to meet you, Dr. Garth," Alex said.

"I'm overrated, but I accept the compliment. I'm told your Isaac's PhD daughter. Are you excited about our mission to Titan?"

"The journey to Titan will be a dream come true."

"Trent, Bryan and Isaac are anxious to hear how the surgery went. Try to get some rest," Michael said.

"How can I rest when I now have complete access to the knowledge buffet?"

They said goodbye and left the lab.

"Michael, I'm in shock. Trent Garth is a part of SEEDS? How did you manage to keep it a secret?"

"My implant."

"Any other miracles you want me to see?"

He looked at his watch.

"We still have time, follow me."

They detoured to another Bioengineering lab. They entered and put on new lab coats, and masks. When the researchers saw them coming they gathered in front of the metal examination table.

"Michael, Alex, what timing. I was about to call you."

Dr. Steven Winslow lead the research team in the lab with a different mission. He was anxious to show Michael what he accomplished 'Outside of the box.'

"You will be surprised, Michael."

"You always surprise me."

"Our Titanauts should have an advantage in order to conquer Titan."

The researchers stepped to the sides of the examination table revealing a male body. Steven showed Michael and Alex an X-ray held up to the light.

"Two hearts?" Alex asked.

"To boost the blood flow for more demanding strenuous situations."

The patient was a young man in his mid-twenties, and one of the flight crew.

"How do you feel, Tommy?"

"I can't describe what a boost of energy I get from the second heart. I feel as if I could run to Titan and back.

"You won't have to run there."

"We've had Tommy on the treadmill, and he wasn't perspiring when he got off."

"What if the second heart fails? What happens to Tommy?" Michael asked.

"He will use one heart and be back in the

simulators practicing drills."

"Remarkable!"

"Impressive! Go slow, Tommy, and don't break one. Is it possible to break *two* hearts?" Alex asked.

"We're late for a meeting with Bryan and Isaac. Take it easy, Tommy," Michael said.

They walked toward the door. Steven shouted more news.

"Biology developed a synthetic skin they say will last for eternity."

As they walked to the elevator, Alex had a technical question.

"The research with Tommy, is it ethical? 'Grinders' use cybernetic devices, I mean, are we 'Biopunks'?"

"We're scientists. What we do is scientific research on techno-progressivism for space travel to preserve, and protect humans. Grinders believe science belongs to everyone, and use it to manage their own biology. They try to create 'after human beings' with technology and altered DNA. It goes back to cyberneticist, Dr. Kevin Warwick's, *Project Cyborg*."

"We're Grinders, aren't we?"

"Yes, we're Grinders."

They said hello to Becca and walked into Isaac's office. Alex gave him a loving embrace.

"Judging from the grins on your faces, you have good news for me. Wait, I'll get Bryan in here."

Isaac used the intercom.

"I'll let Alex tell you about it."

Isaac couldn't be fazed. He'd come to expect the unusual, and the ultra-science.

Bryan walked in and took a seat. Michael sat on the

sofa.

Alex wandered the office while she told them about Trent and Tommy.

"Why didn't you tell me the superstar was here?" she asked.

"Trent and I worked on several theories together at Cambridge back in the day. He was elated when I asked him to join SEEDS and be a test subject. As far as the young man with two hearts, would he still be classified as human? Maybe Human II," Isaac said.

"I'm glad to hear everything went well. Now we can move ahead with our plans," Bryan said.

Alex stared out the window.

"What're you thinking, Alex?"

She paused.

"We're headed into space, farther than anyone has gone. We're going back to our roots as explorers. We'll observe the magnificence of the universe as it passes by the windows of the ship. How fortunate are we?"

"Michael, tomorrow you leave on the company plane to Mission Hills to check on the progress down there with the expansion," Bryan said.

"What time?"

"Early thirty."

"What time is it? What day is it? I haven't been outside SEEDS for days."

The plane's turbofans rotated as Michael approached the plane. Dusk still filled the sky.

Michael's circadian clock's alarm rang, and he kept shutting it off. He climbed the stairs and was met by one of the pilots.

"I'm going to attempt a power nap during the flight."

"We'll be gentle, Dr. Talbot."

His power nap was brief, so he took out the technical drawings to review the changes to the facility. He set them aside, closed his eyes, and ruminated about his "First Contact" with Elan Mason.

His first exposure to SpaceTech was a tour three years before. Inside the massive Mission Hills facility was a SpaceTech Heavy rocket lying horizontal, painted in bright white with red letters, and yellow emergency markings. Twenty-four methane-fueled, cryogenic engines were installed at the business end of the rocket.

"When will she launch?"

"She's already launched from Complex 39-A at KSC. She's scheduled to be stood up on Vandenberg's launch pad next week, the second of three test flights."

"Reusable?"

"Saves tons of money."

Michael was impressed.

In Elan's office was a scale model of his "AIRTran," a clear tube in a racetrack shape.

"In the future, tubes will connect major metropolitan cities. It will reduce the need for commercial aviation, and leave a negligible carbon footprint. With regulated air pressure, instead of jet fuel, the cabin levitates through the tube at speeds of

up to seven hundred KPH. A trip from Los Angeles to San Francisco would take thirty minutes. We can only get the test unit up to three-hundred-fifty KPH, because the tube isn't long and straight. Want to go for a ride?"

"You have an—"

"AIRTran. A scaled down version."

"I would love to ride in it."

Elan drove to the site. After the twelve-minute ride, Michael knew he had met someone special.

The corporate plane landed. Elan met the plane. He noticed Michael was at a low energy level. He took out a small bottle and dumped an all-natural mind enhancer pill into his hand then handed him a bottle of water.

"I use them all the time."

Michael handed Elan the technical drawings he brought.

Entrepreneur, physicist and engineer, Dr. Elan Mason, built a space colonization empire, which was a perfect fit for SEEDS. Both men had visions for the future. Together, they could develop the science and create the hardware.

SpaceTech was years ahead in rocket and propulsion systems. SEEDS was the leader in the development of the internal components. They reviewed the progress made on the EFMs and EFTs.

"Bryan said you have whatever financing you need to expedite the expansion."

"Always good to have financial backing."

They spent six hours discussing the new expansion plans with the architects and engineers. Elan gave them the go ahead for both the Mission Hills, and McGregor facilities.

They drove to his home. For the rest of the day and most of the night, the concept flexing continued, and what their dreams of achievable futuristic concepts were.

"Can the AIRTran be used on Titan?"

"On a moon with a lower air density than Earth's, there would be no need for a tube. All you would need is the track. With tracks on Titan you can accelerate exploration."

"I can't tell you how many times I've looked back to your idea to use SpaceTech Heavy to build the ship by sleeving pre-fabricated, fully-functional ship modules together, instead of transporting parts to construct the ship in the shroud. If we increase production by ten percent, the ship will be completed within a year."

"And then, we are on our way. Launching out of Vandenberg and McGregor, instead of transporting everything to Kennedy saves time and money. For our mission pull, launching from orbit will save fuel and weight."

"Clemons suggested the ANNULAR and VASIMR be added to the aft propulsion modules for experimental runs en route," Michael said.

"My large nozzle SE-15s aren't futuristic, but are more than enough propulsion to take us to Titan. They are tested and proven. For Titan's atmosphere, the short nozzle -15s is all we need to maneuver. The -15s are reliable, but the ANNULAR and VASIMR, if they perform, will give us a solid a backup."

"I like the fact the -15s are fueled with methane, which burns cleaner, and produces higher performance numbers. Titan bathes in methane, so if we want to travel further out there's no limitations."

"Clemons and I had a long talk about other options like Photon Rockets, Laser Sail Push, Fission Drive Propulsion, antimatter, and even warp drive based on Alcubierre's concept of riding on bent space-time. Nuclear thermal propulsion has reliability problems because of the vibrations and excessive heat," Elan said.

"There's always the chance Clemons' engineers, and yours can develop a fusion engine, which would give us speed, and no radiation issue."

"I heard something about a renowned scientist with an implanted microchip in his brain."

"I was about to bring that up. Fulbright was successful implanting it into Trent Garth," Michael said.

"Is it working?"

"Works perfect, I spoke to him right after. He's connected to the combined knowledge of mankind."

"I worked with Trent at MIT. I'm surprised the knowledge wasn't flowing *from* him *to* the computers," Elan said.

"There's another surprise from Bioengineering. Winslow's test subject, one of the crew, now has two human hearts."

"What?"

"He says it will give the colonists extra stamina to work on the moon. He's competing with the Robonaut. Sanders created a 'singularity,' a complete electric motor-hydraulic cyborg, with a quantum computer chip with Sanders' engrams copied to it. The argument is the singularity is the next step in human evolution. There are those who disagree. Bryan and Isaac want to have on board lifeforms born, or artificially created, to see which would better survive on Titan."

"I don't like A.I. I think it's dangerous territory. There's no forecasting, which way the technology will go. Besides, what's the point of humans going to Titan if the robots replace, or subjugate us?"

"Isaac told me to be sure the modules will Autoland on Titan. Also, if the electromagnetic locks and blow bolts on them fail, we'll have to leave them on the ship, and Britte will have to fabricate a space elevator. If that happens, it'll take longer to construct the colony."

"It would be a shame for the colonists to commute from the ship down to Titan, not to mention the extra food storage required. By the way, I want to be the *first* human to set foot on Titan."

"You should be."

Elan raised his glass.

"The other issue is, space debris. Something as small as a pebble could damage the entire ship. The radar we have today is incapable of discerning space dust, particles, or rocks. The engineers suggested a reinforced, high-impact, pointed cone installed at the front of the ship to deflect the debris," Michael said.

"Why not a laser shield able to sense the debris and annihilate it with laser beams? Let's call Hinkle."

"We don't get along."

"I might have better luck with him.

Elan called.

"Bob? Elan, good, how is the most important asset of SEEDS?"

Elan grinned at Michael. He was able to speak Bob's language.

"Bob, about the space debris issue. Yeah, heard about it from Talbot. What? He doesn't like you? I don't think so, he's doing a job. Listen, what about a laser shield able to sense the debris, and annihilate it with laser beams? Think you could put something like that together? Yeah? Sounds good, thanks, Bob, I knew you were the one to talk to."

Hinkle was the master when it came to space communication and navigation. He had a small receiver on his desk still able to contact Voyager 1, which passed through the Keiper Belt on its way to deep space. While his specialty was communications, it didn't carry over to his personal communications. He was never happy unless you weren't.

"He thinks your aloof, Michael, said you only visit the *specialty* labs. He wants your attention."

"Who has time to be aloof?"

The news stations broadcast the deteriorating state of nations. It sent chills up and down spines, and made for an increase in the use of psychotropic medications. Many parents contemplated where they'd find a safe place for their families. The children played, but they were cognizant of mommy and daddy's worries.

Astrophysicists discussed the theory of inflation, not the monetary kind, but the fact the universe had sped up its expansion. The universe moved farther away from Earth.

The board adjusted their timeline.

Chapter 2

Elan and Michael left the next morning on the company plane to San Jose, and SEEDS. They went to Isaac's office to discuss Mission Hills.

"Every day we save will help to assure our departure to Titan. There are dark forces at work in the world right now. I don't want to be here when it hits the fan," Isaac said.

"The changes to Elan's facilities will push us far ahead on our timeline," Michael said.

"I can't tell you how much Bryan and I are grateful for your initiative and drive. I know everyone in this building is working as hard as they can to reach Titan."

"Elan spoke to Bob yesterday. He has him working on a space debris annihilator Elan suggested. Elan can talk with him. I find it difficult," Michael said.

"Are you being aloof again?"

"Why does everyone think I'm aloof?"

"Not everyone, a few."

Elan smiled. Michael changed the subject.

"Where's Alex?"

"She went down to check on Trent about a half hour ago," Isaac said.

"If you see her, tell her Elan and I are headed to

the simulators. John is going to give Elan some stick time for fun. Which reminds me, I want Elan to be the first human to plant feet on Titan."

"Not a problem for me, but I think Dr. Sanders plans the first to stand on Titan will be his Robonaut. I'll tell Alex where you two will be if I see her."

Elan and Michael left for the simulators. As they stepped out of the elevator and into Level 6, they met Britte.

"Michael, Elan, back already?" he asked.

"Too much to do, Phillip," Michael said.

"We developed some new technology you'll like."

"Fabrication is one of my favorite labs," Michael said.

"Tell Bob Hinkle. He stormed into my lab and told me how aloof you are."

"Thirteen months to Titan with Hinkle. I can't wait, maybe I'll stay on Earth and wait for the apocalypse."

"What new things did you develop, Phillip?" Elan asked.

"A more resilient, lighter material called graphene. I can use it with the 10-D printer to create anything from computer screens, to fish farm tanks, to ships windows. I recommend we use it for the sleeves in between the double hull of the ship. The lighter weight means more water carried. Dr. Hammerstein has improved the RG's electromagnetic ammunition. He's developed a projectile, which act more like a shotgun shell for wider dispersal, while maintaining a much higher speed. He also believes he can double the range."

"How does an RG work?" Elan asked.

"The ship stores electricity in a pulsed power system, like our compact fission power generator in the aft EPM compartment. The RG receives an electric burst, or pulse, and it creates an electromagnetic force, which determines how far the projectile will travel from the hyper-velocity. DARPA's RG projectile passed through a multi-Tesla magnetic field. The other advantage to an RG is the safety factor, because we don't need to store gunpowder, which means more cargo space."

"How many will be on the ship?" Mason asked.

"Two, one on top and one on the bottom of the GR," Phillip said.

"Bryan said he gave Hammerstein a special task. Where are we in its development?" Michael asked.

"I'd say talk to him, but he's a man of few, but deliberate words. He developed a laser beam, which directs a bolt of lightning to target."

"A modern-day Tesla," Elan said.

"He's been to the simulators to show Commander Kelly how it works."

"We're headed there next."

"Dr. Patterson perfected a ground-based, short-range GPS system for the colony's farm, and mining equipment. Dr. Wiggins developed a superior human waste receptacle. Dr. Simmons created durable, reliable, flexible, fiber-reinforced hydrogels. Dr. Sanders looked at it for his 'Robonauts,' and Dr. Clifford for medical devices. We've developed highly efficient LEDs, which do not radiate heat, and scrubbers to help remove the ethylene, the gas plants radiate, which leads to plant decay. They also remove bacteria, mold, fungi, mycotoxins, viruses, and odors, which will help keep our Titanauts healthy. We can grow plants aeroponically, which saves on anchoring materials, thereby saving weight and space on the ship. We have an improved hibernation system. Our cryo-beds are *stacked* to save space. We use drawers. They share the 93° temperature, and they won't have to be reset in fourteen days. They use far less power. The sleepers will not have the muscle atrophy non-sleepers do. Lastly, Dr. Rogers came up with a metallic, flexible, compound material, which is stronger than steel. He calls it 'Rogersnite.' We earn our keep here, Michael."

"Yes, you do. Can the new synthetic steel, *Rogersnite*, be used to coat the forward areas of the ship?" Elan asked.

"We planned to use it on the FRMs for added protection. I'm sure we could coat the ship in it."

"Winslow implanted a second heart into one of the crew," Michael said.

"What?"

"Tommy's doing fine. Steven will monitor long-term issues."

"Two hearts still doesn't beat three of a kind," Phillip said.

"Fulbright implanted a transceiver into a test subject," Michael said.

"Amazing. I know Dr. Sanders' singularity is up and running. He asked about the synthetic skin. We've also developed a storage unit for the embryos of humans, and every species of animal, including seeds from every plant, tree, crop, and even flowers."

"Sounds more like an ark than an interplanetary ship," Elan said.

"Clones, whenever I tried it, I always came out a sheep," Phillip said.

Elan laughed. They said goodbye and walked toward the elevators. Michael's phone rang. It was Alex.

"Where are you?"

"On our way to Simulator 3. Commander Kelly found an opening in the training schedule, so he's letting Elan fly the ship."

"I'll meet you there."

A half hour later, Alex entered the simulator. Michael pulled her forward to watch Elan. John guided him into orbit around Titan.

"Now ease forward on the control grip, and watch the PFD here. It's giving you the pitch attitude, and navigational guidance for the approach."

Elan jinked too far left and got frustrated.

"Don't worry about it. It doesn't take but a hairs width of movement on the control grip to make significant changes. Use two fingers to move it, not a death grip. Worst case scenario you can select Auto-Flight, reset the approach, and do it again."

Before signing on with SEEDS, Kelly had a career with DARPA as a test pilot for their top-secret aircraft. He used to divert from his flight plans and mess with the civilian UFO patrols were out searching the skies. Recognized as the best aviator in the world, he had the plaques, awards, commendations, and medals to prove it. He was only twenty-nine years old.

"Better, you see, a light touch goes a long way. Now activate the Auto-Flight to orbit the planet while you prepare for landing."

Elan did better on his second approach.

"It's all we have time for, John, push harder in the planning and training areas. Our launch date moved up," Michael said.

"How did he do, John?" Alex asked.

"I'd fly with him."

Elan climbed out of the seat. John said the next time, he would let him fly into a black hole. Elan's eyes widened.

Fifteen other crew members, and an astrophysicist with an implant able to cite a giga-giga-trillion bits of human knowledge besides his own, would back John up.

Michael called Becca and asked her to tell Isaac they were on their way. Bryan was already in Isaac's office. Alex, Elan, and Michael took a seat on the sofa.

"It been a hard day's night," Isaac said.

Bryan asked for a progress report. Alex gave him one.

Bryan looked at Elan, eyebrows elevated.

"Yes, you can ride in the AIRTran."

"Anything else before we adjourn?" Isaac asked.

"I think we covered it," Michael said.

"Let's go home," Bryan said.

They stood and headed for the door.

"There is one thing we need to discuss, not right

now, but soon," Elan said.

"What did we miss?" Isaac asked.

"We are scientists, and focus on innovations, solving problems, and technology, but have you considered the colonist's life once they're on Titan? Who will be in charge? What are the laws? What type of government?"

They hadn't given it any consideration.

"I have a friend at Stanford, a constitutional lawyer. I'll give him a call and see if he can help."

"Sounds good, Elan."

Alex and Michael were at SEEDS before the others.

"As your assistant, I get all the updates before anyone else does. I'm an *insider*," she said.

"Correct, it's a twenty-four-hour, seven-day-a-week position. Let's move, we have a lot of ground to cover."

"I'm not sure I'm going to like being an insider with *those* hours."

They found Elan in Hammerstein's lab. Elan designed the LDA to work in conjunction with two of the LDCs. When the Large Detector Array picked up any sized object in front of the ship, it sent a signal to the TCU, which directed the LDCs to target. Hammerstein's defensive lasers used a single laser beam. In testing, the system was dead accurate.

Alex, Elan, and Michael entered Robotics.

"I want you to open and close your eyes in the

standard test sequence," Robert said.

Both eyes snapped open and closed. The optical cameras embedded in the eye sockets had a bluish translucent look. The eyes repeated the sequence several times followed by a left to right snap, and then closed again. The command was picked up by the two receivers in Robonaut's shiny dome.

"Now I want you to raise your right arm to a forty-five-degree angle."

The polished-chrome finish with the new synthetic skin, which was able to *feel* because the carbon nanotubes blended into the waffled plastic, sent signals to the Transhuman's memory chip. Robonaut's right arm rose to forty-five degrees and stopped.

"Turn your right hand to the left three-hundred-sixty degrees, and stop, please."

The hand rotated as requested, stopped, and gave Robert the finger. His research assistants, in on the prank, laughed. Robert continued with several command-response protocols. Robonaut operated as designed, and met all parameters. Neuroprosthetics made a connection between the primary neuro cortexes, and the mechanical devices. For the assistants, envy bred sarcasm.

"Dr. Sanders?"

"Yes, Frank?"

"Do you have to say 'please' to make it work?"

Robonaut gave Frank the finger without being commanded. Frank went silent.

Robert wanted the Robonauts to have a significant role in colonizing the planet. They would do the heavy lifting constructing the colony's habitats, and structures. They would be autonomous, but in the event of a problem, they would auto-connect with Sanders for the proper procedures. The Robonaut had an OVERRIDE switch if needed. Robert believed through Robonaut he would live forever as Kurzweil had predicted. Alex and Michael walked into Robert's lab.

"That finger better not have been directed at me," Michael said.

"My assistants pranked me. Thanks for coming down. Alex, good to see you," Robert said.

"Hello, Robert, I'm Michael's assistant."

"Excellent, you won't be as *aloof* as Michael I'm sure."

Michael decided Hinkle spoke to everyone in SEEDS.

"I'm joking, Hinkle stopped in the other day."

"He's the reason I approved of replacing humans with A.I."

"He's different, even I wouldn't replicate him."

"Robonaut looks almost human with the new synthetic skin," Alex said.

"He has what all women want," Robert said.

"What's that?"

"A switch to turn him off."

"I like him already. Will there be a Miss Robonaut?"

"If they learn to replicate. Michael, Robonaut has passed all its primary tests with a basic copy of my brain. Thurgood will download a complete copy next."

"You can tell the size of a man by the size of his microchip," Alex said.

They laughed.

"We wanted to check on your progress, Robert. We're headed to Medical."

They walked to Biology and Space Medicine.

"Dr. Baker, do you have everything you need for the ship?" Michael asked.

"Yes, everything and more, thank you," Clifford said.

Clifford handed Michael the layout he designed for the medical modules. He also gave him a list of supplies ready to be taken on board the ship; cardiac heart monitors, pulse oximeters, central venous catheters, intravenous tubes, chest tubes, endotracheal tubes, ventilators, and various life support devices. Innovative precision medical tools, and biological-computing systems, which dispensed nanotech pills for illnesses, and to provide accurate diagnosis were also boxed and ready. The operating theater had yet to be installed. Clifford also coordinated with Cryogenics because it was his responsibility to monitor the cryo-beds, and VOE.

"Anything we forgot?" Alex asked.

"No, I have great nurses and medical specialists to work with. We're ready to move to the ship." Clifford said.

"Good, we still need to do psychological, and physical exams on everyone before we send them up. We need to be certain no one has any viruses, or illnesses, we can't handle, even if it means they stay behind."

"My two best nurses are preparing screening."

"I never have to worry about Medical, Alex."

"Noted."

"Elan brought in a constitutional law professor from Stanford who's giving a lecture on suggested colonial law."

"Did you want to attend?" Michael asked.

"We missed it, but I'd like to hear what he said from someone who attended," Alex said.

They went to Level 1 and the conference room where the lecture was held. Elan walked out of the room with the professor.

"Alex, Michael, this is Dr. Robert Goldman. You missed an excellent lecture. Michael is our Project Manager and Alex is Isaac's daughter."

"Nice to meet you, Dr. Goldman. It's Alexandra, but I go by Alex. Dad wanted a son."

"I told, Dr. Goldman, it should be a 'direct democracy,' no Congress, Supreme Court, a three-person board, and not an Executive Branch. The colonists will face significant issues on Titan. They should wake in the morning, and view the issues on their computers where they can vote after passing a retinal scan. I suggested religion be practiced in the home, not as a community, eliminating any domination by denomination," Elan said.

"Sounds functional," Alex said.

"Elan thinks of things we never did before. You are invited, Dr. Goldman, to go with us to Titan," Michael said.

"I'll consider your offer, Michael."

Elan walked Goldman to the doors, said

goodbye.

He took a seat at the conference table with Bryan, Isaac, Alex, Michael, and John.

"Michael, let's review our progress to date," Bryan said.

"SEEDS-2025 is just shy of one kilometer in length, fifty-five meters wide. Modules 1, 2, and 3 contain the flight deck and crew quarters. A work station with a dome has been installed above the flight deck for Trent to work in. Module 3, 4, 5, and 6 contain the Medical Station. Module 7 has the stacked cryo-beds with the VOEs stored above them. Fourteen Titanauts desire to sleep their way to Titan. I recommend we surprise them by leaving them behind. I *highly* recommend Bob Hinkle should be in one. Food Service is in Modules 8, 9, 10, and 11 next to the cryo-beds so they can share the refrigeration. The SEEDS' Colonist's Agreement states, 'Colonists are required, in the event of need, to save the colony by surrendering their flesh for food.' I thought we should dine on the frozen dinners first."

Bryan dragged a palm across his face. Isaac smiled at Alex. Isaac smiled at Alex.

"Next are Modules 12, and 13 where our cargo, including two Robonauts, are stored. Beyond cargo, Modules 15, 16, and 17 is the EPM. The BCS, 10-Ds, and the compact nuclear fission reactor, MegaPower, is next to the engineering quarters."

Isaac looked across at Elan, his eyebrows raised.

"The SE–1 is in the last module of the ship. SE–2, and SE–3 are inside two external modules attached to the underbelly of the ship. Our ever-vigilant engineers can work on the three large-nozzle Se-15s from below the EPM, including tunes ups, spark plugs, and oil changes with a filter."

"Michael, you hurt me when you talk about my engines like that," Elan said.

"I have a deep affection for your SE–15s, Elan. The ANNULAR and VASIMR rest on tracks, so they can be positioned easily for testing or use."

Alex tried to hide her yawn.

"The EFTs extend from the back of the FRMs to the aft end of the ship, each has electromagnetic locks and blow bolts. Of the three small-nozzle, maneuvering Se-15s, one is below the flight deck, and the other two are on either side of the ship. Each FRM has maneuvering air-pressure thrusters, and an Autoland system."

"Is there room to land SEEDS-2025 on Titan?" Isaac asked.

"Yes, we selected a sixty-kilometer-wide crater we named Base Crater. After SEEDS–2025 is on Titan, the colonists will remain on board until the structures are complete. The engineers will verify the structures are powered by the fission generator, and the fish farm and fresh water tank are operational."

"It's to our advantage to land the ship, but conditions may not allow it. I'll review the progress of the first FRM landing from the Shuttle. If it looks like we can set the ship down, I will advise John," Elan said.

"The decision to land can't be made any sooner," John said.

"Continuing, the exterior surfaces of the ship have been coated in *Rogersnite*, a translucent synthetic steel," Michael said.

"Status of the GR?" Bryan asked.

"The Gravity Ring was anchored to the ship three days ago by four massive pylons, two of them have elevators. Inside the GR are the working labs, hydroponics, the fish farm tank, a computer center, a virtual golf course, a G-pool lane, a theater, conference room, recreational areas, a gym, an eBook library, and a small garden next to the Observation Deck's large portal," Michael said.

"Weapons systems?" Bryan asked.

"The ship has three LDCs and one LDA. The LDA sends signals to the TCU, which in turn fires the LDC above the flight deck. The other two mounted LDCs are on the GR opposite one Rail Gun on top, and one on the bottom," John said.

"Have the colonists received their training?" Bryan asked.

"All but two, you, and Isaac," Alex said.

"Please tell them about the jumpsuits, I'm about talked out," Michael said.

"Each colonist will receive two color-coded jumpsuits representing their group. The jumpsuits are self-cleaning, and transmit current health status to Medical. They are allowed one duffle bag of personal items," Alex said.

Elan leaned forward, elbows on the table.

"What do I tell my personnel regarding making the flight?" Elan asked.

"How many are there?" Isaac asked.

"Two-hundred-six plus me."

"The answer is to make enough FRMs to house them, and add an extra EFM with additional provisions, so we can take them along. We need all the colonists we can get on Titan," Isaac said.

"What if we build another ship, SEEDS–2025A, for my personnel? It won't have to carry the equipment, and a GR like SEEDS–2025 does," Elan said.

"You decide, Elan, how to proceed. You know Isaac and I will fund it. Just don't cause a delay for SEEDS-2025."

"The engineers are ready for the -15 test runs. They're also testing every mechanical device to make sure they're operational. The cabin pressure checks still need to be done. I'd make them move faster, but I don't want them to miss something, or make a mistake," John said.

"I concur, questions, comments?" Bryan asked.

None.

"You all have done good work, thank you," Isaac said.

A month passed.

Bryan and Isaac stood in front of their personnel. A camera focused on them ready to broadcast across closed circuit to monitors. Those in Mission Hills and McGregor put they work aside.

"Due to the critical political atmosphere, we have made changes to our timeline. The U.S.S

SEEDS–2025 will launch three weeks from today. By the end of the week, you must have your affairs in order. Beginning next week, we will send the flight crew to prepare the ship for departure. Once we get word the ship is ready to leave for Titan, we will begin to transport you up in the order of essential, and non-essential personnel. The fully-automated Phoenix Shuttle, which has room for thirty passengers, will take you to the ship," Bryan said.

John would leave to prepare the ship for launch much sooner than expected. He would have the help, and wisdom, of a well-trained crew, and Trent Garth. What they learned on the first flight would be the blueprint, the textbook guide, for additional flights SEEDS–2025 made.

It sunk in he had seven days to be with John, Sr. His mom passed away ten years earlier. He had no siblings.

He pushed the glass doors open on Level 1 and walked to his car. He loved his dad more than anything in the world. He sat in his car as the tears fell. He didn't try to stop them. If they fell in the car, they might not fall in front of his dad. He backed away from the massive hangar, waved at the guard at the gate, and headed home. He detoured to a store to get hot dogs and beer. He needed to solidify memories to take with him to Titan. He arrived home and they took the bags into the house. They took two cold brews to the back porch and settled in to their favorite chairs.

"Do you think War World Last is on the horizon?"

John wasn't thinking about war.

"What do you think, Son?"

John drank from the bottle.

"What is it about a cold beer on a hot summer day?"

"What is it? It's the best thing about summer," John, Sr. said.

John took another drink.

"World War Last, what if World War—"

"Nothing I can do about it. What I can do is sit on the back porch, enjoy the fresh air, and be with you."

John, Sr. read John's mood.

"They moved up the launch date. I leave in six days to get the ship ready."

John, Sr.'s eyes moistened.

"I didn't expect this conversation for a few more years."

"Caught me by surprise too, Dad."

Cary Allen Stone

Chapter 3

The first Phoenix Shuttle carried the crew to SEEDS–2025. As they approached, Commander Kelly did a preflight of the ship's exterior. The bright spotlights illuminated the ship. Detailed drawings of SEEDS–2025 could not compare to what he saw. John took in the view of his ship. As an aviator, he would bond with it, come to know its beauty, and imperfections, not unlike a lover. He would not see her from such a vantage point until he landed her on Titan if able, so he committed it to memory. Once the Phoenix Shuttle docked, John boarded first through the airlock. The engineers greeted him as he stepped onto the ship. The crew followed, everyone's heart skipped a beat, except for Tommy's which skipped two beats. Reality set in. John and Trent went straight to the flight deck.

John looked over the instrumentation. He placed his hand on the TCs and the LDC switches. He located the communication and navigation transmitters and receivers. Trent climbed the steps to his workstation and looked out the dome.

"Isn't space magnificent?"

Trent made a radio check with Flight Monitoring.

Each crew member wore a lightweight boot, which would automatically lock magnetically to the floor if the artificial gravity failed. They wore the new NASA spacesuits.

John told them to pick out their quarters and store their gear.

After, they followed him through the ship to familiarize themselves with their new home.

First Officer Rhian Estefan made notes on items that needed attention before launch. Pressure bulkheads, separated all modules. They inspected the Medical Station then entered the stacked cryo-bed and VOE module. The beeping monitors were the only sounds they heard there, unless a FAIL alarm wailed. They walked through Food Service and the cargo module. Each stared at the seven-foot-tall Robonauts. The EPM had limited space, so they went in one at a time.

The crew split in two and raced both elevators to the GR. They gathered on the Observation Deck, and looked back at the Earth through the floor to ceiling portal. If anyone felt conflicted about leaving, the view convinced them to stay.

"If any of you have decided this ship isn't for you, please say so now, so you can return on the Phoenix Shuttle," John said.

"It's too early to mutiny, John," Brenda said.

Their familiarization tour of the GR continued, all were surprised at how spacious the area was.

"We should run some checks on the flight deck," John said.

They headed back, Rhian taking notes.

On the flight deck, John heard Trent requesting implant updates.

"Need anything, Trent?"

"I need to settle down before I hyperventilate. Being on the ship is *stimulating*."

"Last chance, anyone have a change of heart?"

Tommy raised his hand, but only John knew he had two hearts. He would keep an eye on him until Dr. Winslow boarded.

"I want *all* crew positions to check *all* systems. I want each of you to sit at your station, and get a feel for being on the actual ship, instead of the simulator. When you're comfortable in those positions, trade seats, so you can be up to speed on backup."

John believed the interiors of the ship's modules were utilitarian, but comfortable. The ergonomics of each flight position was perfect.

Michael radioed John.

"How do you like the ship?"

"The flight deck looks exactly like the simulator. The artificial gravity feels good. All the exterior navigation lights are on, so the Russians, and Chinese can stare in envy."

"Oh, they're staring all right. You have six days to get familiar with the ship, and complete your systems checks. After we get a 'Checks Complete' notification, we'll send up the Titanauts. Enjoy your new home, John. How about your crew? Anyone change their mind?"

"There goes my confidence level. Michael, would you give my dad a call and tell him everything's fine."

"I already spoke to him. He said 'Godspeed, John

Kelly.' He's so proud of you."

"Thanks, Michael, leaving him behind is the hardest part. I'm sure the ship will feel like home soon."

John ordered the Shuttle to go back. He led the crew through repeated checks on every computer, flight control, and switch in the cockpit. He initiated random simulated emergencies. The engineers worked with the crew on the SE–15's final checks.

In days, they would depart on the long journey to Titan. John would command "Engines ON." He looked through the forward windows, and saw the open arms of an exciting universe.

What, or who, is waiting out there for us?

Titan is the largest of the sixty-two known moons in orbit around Saturn. The cosmologists said it was the best place to colonize according to the information they received from the Cassini spacecraft, and Huygens Probe, both orbited Saturn for thirteen years observing its rings, and moons. The Cassini spacecraft cut through Titan's thick haze with infrared cameras and radar, and launched the Huygens probe onto Titan, which provided statistics, and the first visuals of the moon.

Titan's unbreathable atmosphere is a mixture of 95% methane, and 5% nitrogen. The surface is encrusted by rocks, patches of ice, dunes around the moon's equator, and precipitous shorelines around methane lakes. Its *cryovolcanos* eject methane, liquid water, and ammonia creating the landforms. The moon, like Earth, has seasons.

More important was the revelation from Cassini and Huygens of massive, stable, underground oceans 100

KM below the surface, seas of hydrocarbons, which could support life.

The Titanauts would encounter an average temperature of -179° Celsius, and Titan days equal to sixteen Earth days. Working a half day on Titan meant a shift of eight Earth days.

John was the ship's commander and an available captain. With him were co-captains, Brenda Holder, and Hunter Ragsdale.

They would be tested by the unimaginable, and had to find immediate, and lasting answers to all crises. If a problem arose, detrimental to the ship, all three captains, and Trent, would apply crew concept to determine the best course of action. Each was new to space flight, and the situations they hadn't trained for required as much input as possible. What they learned en route would be written into the Flight Manual for future explorations.

The lives on the ship, besides their own, they held in each of their hands. It was a heavy responsibility, and they stayed on high alert.

The First Officers were Lukas Easton, Rhian Estefan, and Sean McNeal. Each of them had also checked out in the simulator as backup captains. Keeping an eye on the many flight computers and systems were the SCNOs, Edward Kingston, Susan Wright, and Hank Stillwater. Each could dismantle and rebuild the computers on the flight deck. All crew members had weapons training, but the four WCSs, Danny Chan, Tommy Maxwell, Ricky Tinsdale, and George TwoBears were the warriors. They were confident, yet cautious. Brave, but not fearless.

They would also rely heavily on the input of Trent. His judgment calls could be the difference between a successful mission, and a devastating failure. Crew reports back to Flight Monitoring would carry weight with the engineers for Elan's ship.

The crew had become a family during their extensive training. During the first free time they had, they were all, but quiet. Over the ship's speakers, Lukas played Holst's, *The Planets, Saturn, the Bringer of Old Age*. Ricky, the antagonist, rolled his eyes.

"This will be a longer flight than I imagined."

"I want to hear *Stairway to Heaven*," Brenda said.

She was a free spirit. The wild streaks of primary colors in her hair distracted from her razor-sharp intellect and wit.

"No, not *Stairway*, *Dream On* because being here has fulfilled all of my dreams," Susan said.

She was the most impulsive of the crew. She wore a special amulet to protect her during the journey.

"You *could* play some Marley to take away the stress, man," Edward said.

A native of Jamaica, Edward was laid back, but had a presence. He knew the journey was long, and there was no better way to de-stress.

"I can't believe we're on the first ship. I wanted this bad, but I was sure something would mess it up," Hunter said.

John was proud of them. They had accomplished much. If they completed the mission, they would be heroes. If they failed, they would perish in the deep cold of space. SEEDS would have failed its mission, and they would be responsible.

"I have a question, and I'd like an honest answer from each of you," Sean said.

It was in his disposition to maintain intense eye contact. At first, it made the others uncomfortable, but over time, they no longer noticed.

"Are any of you afraid right now?" Sean asked.

Glances crossed the space.

"I would be a fool to say no. It's a violent universe," John said.

"If I get scared I might soil my flight suit. How will I live it down?" Ricky asked.

After the laughter subsided, they took turns and acknowledged their own fears, but also spoke of how excited they were to explore the solar system, and Titan.

"I have a question about something we never addressed in training. If we encounter aliens, are they aliens if they're out in space?" Ricky asked.

They loved his humor.

"Are we the aliens out here?" Rhian asked.

"Ricky was an alien on Earth," Susan said.

She was a test case for the new Biolens Implant, a pair of repeater transmitters for the flight computers, and the system status indicators. The lens was basically a HUD.

Ricky accepted the responsibility of keeping their minds off the dangerous journey.

"I have a question. Are any of you secret androids with plans to divert SEEDS–2025 to a beacon signal, so we can be killed by an alien monster with serious dental issues?"

He felt a pair of hands around his neck. George's way of saying "Enough."

A full-blooded Native-American, George had an intellect to rival the other scientists on board. He graduated first in his class from CAL-TECH with a degree in astrophysics and mechanical engineering. He was selected for WCS because he served on the Navy's Seal Team 6, Special Weapons.

"What happens if one of our Robonauts doesn't want to play nice with us?" Sean asked.

"I'll handle them," Tommy said.

Tommy had two sledgehammer arms from spending hours in gyms.

"They say the A.I.'s will replace humans. All I can say is, *we're* flying this ship," Brenda said.

"No, we *monitor* the A.I. systems controlling the ship. They think faster than any of us. We're old technology," Sean said.

"They have manual override on them," Danny said.

"Yeah, we practiced in the simulators, but this is the real world, or better yet the real *outer world*," Sean said.

"Tell Engineering to loosen the Robonauts' nuts, so they won't be aggressive," Ricky said.

"They're not even powered up, so leave them alone," Rhian said.

Hank read a crime fiction novel, and let the others do the talking. If you needed a good listener, he was your priest, minister, or analyst.

"The only one to watch is the Sanders Robonaut,

not your do as I command robot," Lukas said.

"I think we covered the rogue robot scenario," John said.

"We should prepare for our travelers, make it a smooth transition for them. This is home for the next year and change, so let's make it a happy home," Brenda said.

High-fives went around.

One of the rigid rules on the ship stated, "Titanauts and crew are restricted from on board romances, and the bearing of offspring." They all signed the agreement, which was intended to prevent distractions from duty. When they occupied the colony, they were free to fall in love, and start families.

The first Titanauts had completed their training, psychological, and physiological testing was complete. They stood before Bryan and Isaac prepared to board the Phoenix Shuttle to LEO, and the ship.

Each GL was responsible to acclimatize their group to the ship in a brief time. They assigned the order of departures on the Phoenix Shuttle, and the quarters in the FRMs. Each group assigned to a GL wore the same colored jumpsuits with the SEEDS logo patch, and embroidered names.

The first to leave on the Phoenix Shuttle were a hybrid, cross section of the scientists, researchers, and engineers needed most.

Bryan and Isaac spoke to them.

"This day came much faster than we all imagined. Look where you're headed, outer space to a new world. You will conquer Titan. Everything you do, and learn, will be passed down through generations. You will one day find your names listed in the new history books. Be safe, be strong, and never stop believing in our dream."

They applauded until Isaac spoke.

"I will never forget this moment. I look at your faces, and see the excitement in your eyes. I'm proud of you, and our work here at SEEDS. You are the best, and the brightest stars we have, and we want you to shine."

Michael spoke.

"Now, take your things. Your GLs will transport you on the bus to the Phoenix Shuttle launch pad."

The colonists gathered like children going on a school field trip.

As they boarded the Phoenix Shuttle, each stopped to look back at SEEDS and the landscape. The apprehension was replaced with adrenaline. They had flown on commercial airlines. What they saw up to thirty-thousand feet didn't impress them. After fifty-thousand feet, they saw the curvature of the Earth until the blue sky turned to black space. As the Shuttle continued toward the ship, things they had in their possession rose in negative gravity. They snatched them back as fast as frogs tongued flies.

When the ship came into view, it became as silent as space inside the Shuttle.

"What a magnificent sight," Fulbright said.

The next sound they heard was the Shuttle's pressure thrusters. SEEDS-2025 dwarfed the Shuttle. Once it docked, they heard a recording.

"Ladies and gentlemen, thank you for flying the Phoenix Shuttle. We hope you plan to use our Phoenix Shuttles for all your space travel needs."

The colonists laughed as they waited for the airlock's green light assuring the airlock was pressurized and safe. The hatch opened, and the first Titanauts set foot on the ship, each greeted by the crew. Fulbright went straight to the flight deck to check on Trent.

Once they all had passed through the airlock, the Phoenix's hatch, and the ship's hatch auto-locked closed. The airlock depressurized, the empty Phoenix Shuttle separated from the ship, and descended back to Earth.

The last Shuttle of the day brought Michael and Alex.

After they dropped off their duffle bags off in the FRMs, the GLs gave them a tour of the ship, including how the emergency gear worked, and what not to touch. After, they were fee to wander unescorted.

Gene, in Flight Monitoring, radioed the ship.

"If you look out the windows, in about twenty minutes, the Russian ship will pass on its way to Mars. We expect the Chinese will depart for Mars early tomorrow morning. They have a better propulsion system, so it will truly be a space race, Flight Monitoring, out."

Brenda announced the Russian fly-by to the colonists. The curious wanted to see what the Russians had created for their flight to Mars. All they saw was a bright white light that appeared to fly at the ship. It was the fastest object in the night sky.

Michael and Alex's quarters were side by side and located close to the flight deck. They settled in. After dinner, they took a walk around the ship. Alex locked her arm through his.

"We should connect our quarters into one large one."

"I'll speak to the engineers."

The automated circadian day turned to circadian night.

John tried to sleep, but the launch ran through his head all night.

Brenda read as a distraction, because she kept thinking they forgot something.

Lukas read his notes, so he wouldn't miss a thing.

Edward slept like a baby.

Gene radioed SEEDS–2025, and asked for a systems status the next morning. Lukas verified the launch numbers.

John sat in the command chair. Brenda sat in the pilot's seat, and Edward checked systems, and fired back answers. It was not the simulator. It was real.

The rest of the crew watched from the back of the flight deck.

The bus took the last thirty Titanauts to the Phoenix Shuttle. Elan was in his office in Mission Hills. Bryan,

Isaac, Becca, John, Sr., and three Flight Monitors stayed to close SEEDS down before taking the next Shuttle.

Earth had been able to coexist in harmony with the animal and plant kingdoms, and the footsteps of the original humans. For the past century, Earth struggled to accommodate the weight of tens of billions of humans. The population required seventy-nine percent more food and energy. Concrete and steel cities covered every inch of its surface without regard for the effect on water reserves. Farmers overharvested the land, and used chemicals, which burned the fields. Toxic chemicals dumped into the rivers led to heavy metal poisoning from arsenic, mercury, and lead. Laws to protect the environment, and population went unenforced.

Animals and plants went extinct. Evolved superbugs, and bacteria resistant to medicines, prevailed. The World Health Organization could not keep up with the plagues.

Energy sources, both fossil fuels, and renewables were exhausted, landmasses decimated. Copper, zinc, and platinum were stripped from the Earth, and depleted in decades. Industrial waste polluted the air and water.

Climate change warnings went unheeded until noxious deadly carbon dioxide gas levels raised at an alarming rate in the atmosphere. Sea levels rose drowning cities along the eastern seaboard.

Wildfires ravaged California. The intensities and frequencies of tsunamis, floods, volcanic eruptions, earthquakes, and melting icebergs took Earth into a downward spiral the likes of a barren Mars.

Humans believed technology would save them, but the artificial intelligent machines made humans obsolete. Cyberwar attacked and disabled cybersecurity.

Humans lost their way, lost anything to believe in, and for some, lost the desire to live. Suicide rates spiked. Any hopes and dreams parents had for their children dissolved. Religious leaders made desperate attempts to ease the suffering, but found ancient doctrines were no longer an answer. They were unable to convince the flock to be compassionate, and help one another. Xenophobia reached epic heights, as did genocide, and filicide. Doomsday Preppers chose to burrow into underground shelters with stored food to wait for the Apocalypse.

Primitive weapons found by archaeologists in wastelands, and under shopping malls, said humans learned to fight to survive early on. Battles were fought over land, money, women, and honor. Over millennia, the winners would become the losers, and the losers would become the winners. War became a human necessity, a learned trait, which only pushed the species closer to extinction. There were those who saw the bloodshed as counterproductive. They believed cooperation would help humans build a better life. They sought a reasoned logic for human existence. They believed humanity wasn't supposed to tear down, but to build up, to orchestrate a better symphony with the Earth. They chose not to fight, but were eradicated by the aggressors. Humans, like rats, followed crazed leaders into the abyss. Wars between belligerent nations scarred the Earth. Darwinian super-predators terrorized the weak, and frail.

World governments remained on constant high alert, prepared to launch their arsenals of nuclear warheads. The warheads, detonated above and below the Earth, released radiation into the Jetstream, which carried the radiation over the entire Earth. The radiation lingered and caused slow, painful deaths. It accounted for the increase in cancers and birth defects.

Philosophers and artists accepted humans were a failed species. Scientists recalled Carl Sagan's warning, "Extinction is the rule. Survival is the exception."

While extinction crept closer, there were those who rushed to find solutions. It took years to prove whether their theories were plausible. A chosen group found viable solutions using the current technology. The answer, they concluded, was no longer to repair Mother Earth, but to leave Earth, and find a new home for humans.

Bryan, Isaac, and Elan saw the future doom of humanity. They decided to be aggressive, and prepare to take humans to the stars, escape extinction.

A rogue nation provoked several countries by launching test ICBMs in their direction. When the rogue nation's engineers and scientists developed nuclear warheads able to reach the East Coast of the U.S., the rogue threatened to incinerate the United States. Supportive nations for each of the belligerents said they would put a dog in the fight. Humans were forced to live in constant fear of a third world war, wherein even the cockroaches wouldn't survive.

Chapter 4

Civil Defense warnings wailed.

The rogue nation launched its warheads. The President entered the launch codes, and launched every nuclear warhead in the US arsenal, including from nuclear-armed submarines. Designated targets vaporized.

Other nations monitored the launches then launched their arsenals. Warheads crisscrossed the skies, too many to destroy before impact. Mushroom clouds rose over every mile on Earth.

Startled citizens watched the warheads rain down. What no one believed would ever happen, had. Few above ground were left alive, buildings collapsed. The landscape was decimated. Billions of irradiated carcasses lay rotting on the scorched Earth beneath the thick, dark atmosphere. The human dinosaurs were eradicated, the Earth sterilized. All living species, including the roaches, went extinct.

Bryan, Isaac, Becca, John, Sr., and the Flight Monitors took the emergency elevator to a secure bunker beneath Level 7 inside SEEDS. They had emergency communications available.

Sacramento took a hit. Military bases up and down each coast were hit. Washington, D.C. was obliterated. The President's bunker took a direct hit.

Elan heard the Civil Defense warnings and watched the reports by the only operational broadcast stations. He looked out of his office and saw mushroom clouds rising in the east. He knew if he didn't act fast, he would die. He donned the new radiation-protective spacesuit, an operational sample from NASA, hanging in his office. He took several oxygen packs, connected one to the suit, and the others he placed into a cart. He contacted SEEDS.

"Bryan, how many are left?"

"Seven, our last thirty colonists were killed while boarding the Shuttle."

"Nellis was hit a few minutes ago. Another one hit east of the mountain range. My people are dead, or will be soon. When they do hit Vandenberg, Mission Hills will be gone. I'm in the sample spacesuit from NASA, and I have three portable oxygen bottles."

"We have RAD gear here. If we go outside, I don't know how long we'll live."

"Have you contacted the ship?"

"We're trying to reach them right now. I'm not sure the radiation hasn't wiped out communications to the ship."

"Bryan, I have a smaller shuttle here in one of the hangers. It only seats six, but it will make it to the ship. We used it for the ISS. I'm coming to get to you. Be ready to evacuate when I call from the tarmac in front of SEEDS. We have a chance to make it to the ship. I'm leaving now!"

Contact with Elan was lost. Bryan looked at the others as they put on the RAD suits.

"SEEDS–2025, do you copy Flight Monitoring?"

No answer. Sean heard a scratchy call on the comm radio, but couldn't confirm.

"John, I think I heard a call from Flight Monitoring, but it was unreadable."

"Confirmed, Commander, I heard it clear on my channel," Trent said.

Sean boosted the signal. Another call came. They heard Bryan's voice.

"SEEDS-2025, I say again, do you copy Flight Monitoring?"

Sean answered.

"We copy, Flight Monitoring, we're ready for the—"

"Get John on the frequency!"

Everyone on the flight deck heard the extreme stress in Bryan's voice.

"Go ahead, Bryan, it's John."

"John, a world war is in progress. Every nation launched. The last colonists to transport up in the Shuttle were killed. Elan radioed from Mission Hills. His people are all dead. He has a smaller shuttle SpaceTech used for the ISS. He's attempting to bring it here. We're down in the bunker below Level 7. We're in RAD suits. When, or if, Elan makes it here, we'll try to reach the ship. Copy?"

Trent verified a nuclear war was in progress. The crew strained to look out the windows.

"Copy all, Bryan, we will stand by for your arrival.

We'll leave the channel open. Good luck, Bryan."

He didn't get an answer. He wasn't sure if they had been hit, until Bryan called back a minute later.

"John, track the shuttle. If you see us coming, be ready to launch, but if you lose our track, launch, and get as far from Earth as you can. Watch out for the ISS, the Russians own it now. Consider them hostile, understood?"

"Copy, Bryan."

"Trent?"

"Yes, John?"

"Are you go for launch?"

"Yes, John."

"Engines ON."

The crew shouted replies with anxious voices. John sent the rest of the crew to perform a walkthrough of the entire ship, and to brief the GLs, but not the colonists. The GLs rushed their people to the FRMs, and checked they were secured in their harnesses. The engineers sat at consoles in the EPM, and heard the command for "Engines ON."

John had Michael and Alex brought to the flight deck. He explained what happened. Michael's mind raced. Alex couldn't believe every living thing on Earth perished, and her dad was in a bunker.

"Are you okay?" Michael asked.

"I will never be okay, it's insane, Michael!"

"Sometimes dreams come true, even the bad ones."

"Flight Monitoring, I say again, Flight Monitoring, do you copy?"

Sean kept transmitting. Thirty-two long minutes passed before Flight Monitoring answered.

"SEEDS–2025, Gene, over."

Relief swept the crew.

"Gene what's the status of the Shuttle?"

There was a painful long pause.

"More ICBMs have hit closer to us, John. Alan arrived about twenty minutes ago. They all departed. You should be able to track their progress now."

"Trent, have you got them?"

"Yes, climbing through fifty-two thousand feet."

"Captain Holder, once the shuttle locks onto the airlock, Departure Checklist."

"Understood, Commander."

"Gene why aren't you on the shuttle?"

"Simple math, John, six seats, seven people. I volunteered to stay."

"We'll send the Shuttle back for you!"

"Too late, John, an ICBM breached SEEDS. I have third-degree radiation burns over eighty percent of my body. I broke open the first aid kit, and gave myself two shots of morphine. You get the ship to Titan."

"Gene—"

Silence for a minute then Gene struggled to speak.

"John...what happened today...is what Bryan, and Isaac saw when they looked...into the future. If no one got to the ship... John, help Elan...he lost all of his people."

The pain was more intense than the morphine could handle.

"Godspeed, John, Flight Moni—"

They received no more transmissions from SEEDS.

Trent called out the distance from the shuttle to SEEDS–2025 using the LMI.

"Three meters from SEEDS, two, one, docked."

A noticeable bump against the ship confirmed it. Tommy verified the pressure was equalized in the airlock then reached across to open the Shuttle's hatch. He pulled them all into the ship.

"We have them, Commander."

They were safe on SEEDS–2025.

Alex threw her arms around Isaac.

"Thank God, I was afraid I lost you."

Isaac didn't stop telling Alex he loved her.

Dr. Baker escorted them to the Medical Station.

"Departure Checklist," Hunter said.

Brenda's hand rested on the synchronized TCs. She turned to look at John, her eyes intense.

"Systems check, Mr. Kingston."

"Green lights across all panels."

"Departure Checklist."

"Complete."

"Set TCs to ninety-five percent."

Brenda pushed them forward and the ship surged. John looked out the forward windows.

Because of the enormity of space, it was difficult to get a sense of the thrust from the SE–15's, except for the G-push into their seats.

As the ship accelerated, it became quiet on the flight deck.

Each crew member lost loved ones. It sunk in deep. They struggled to concentrate on their duties. John had to keep them focused.

"Engine parameters, First Officer."

"All within parameters, Commander."

"Edward, what are you showing on the panels?"

"All green, Commander."

"I'll make the announcement when we get further out."

John knew the colonists sat in abeyance not knowing what had taken place, and why. He had to maintain a command atmosphere, yet be sensitive to the trauma they suffered.

"This is Commander Kelly. I'm sure you're wondering why you're inside your quarters. I will release you in a moment. I'm afraid I have some tragic news. A full-scale nuclear war broke out on Earth. We are unable to confirm if there were any survivors. Bryan, Isaac, Elan, and three others were able to use SpaceTech's Shuttle to reach us. The last Titanauts scheduled to leave on the Phoenix Shuttle were killed."

He let them have a moment.

"I need each of you to remain as clear-headed as possible. I know how difficult it will be. We must stay focused on our mission. The crew and GLs will answer your questions, and assist you as best they can. You're now free to leave your quarters."

The doors opened. No one spoke.

Baker and his medical providers were prepared to treat them for shock. The colonists conversed in low volumes about what John said. Several went to the Observation Deck to try and see what was left of Earth.

In Medical, the six survivors spoke about the billions of lives lost.

Isaac's hands shook. His breathing became irregular. Dr. Baker made him lie down.

"We're lucky we reached the ship. Where's Elan? He was supposed to come here first," Isaac said.

"He's the sole survivor of SpaceTech. It will take some time for him to recover," Michael said.

"Elan is a hero. He lost everything, and saved our lives. If it wasn't for his heroics, I would never have held Alex again."

"We must keep focus, Isaac, we made it into space, we did it the hard way, but we're here," Bryan said.

John went back to check on them.

"Dad, are you okay?"

"A little shaken up, Son, I'll be all right. I'm with you."

He wept. John wrapped his arms around him.

"Thank you, Michael."

"How are you, Mr. Kelly?" Michael asked.

"I need to lie down. I feel light-headed."

Baker helped him onto the examination table and placed a nasal cannula on him.

"I'm glad you made it to the ship, Mr. Kelly," Alex said.

"At what cost? Gene's life? He was a young man with his entire life ahead of him."

John consoled him.

"All of you take it slow. Between what happened on Earth, and new to being in space, give yourselves a chance to adjust," Clifford said.

"If anyone did survive, it won't be long before they perish from the radiation in the atmosphere, the poisoned water, or because there's no food. All they can do is wait to die," Bryan said.

Elan entered.

"How are you, Elan," Isaac asked.

"You saved our lives," Bryan said.

"Because of SEEDS, you saved mine. I need to work. I'll be in the EPM. I want to see how the engines are performing."

He turned to leave.

"John, tell them about Gene," Michael said.

"Gene radioed to say you left in the shuttle. SEEDS was breached, and he suffered severe radiation burns. The morphine shots he took lasted until he passed. His last words were, 'Godspeed, John.'"

Silence.

"We need to get the GLs together, and organize a memorial service for Gene, and all those who perished today," Bryan said.

"I need to get back to the flight deck. Dr. Baker, please keep me posted about my dad."

John entered the flight deck.

"Status report, Captain."

"Ships performing better than expected, Commander."

Brenda watched the speed creep up to 220,000 KPH.

"I want the next scheduled crew to get some sleep before their duty time."

"How do we sleep after the biggest heartbreak of our lives?" Susan asked.

"Find a way. You have a responsibility to all of us to be alert during your duty time."

John, a seasoned aviator, knew how it worked. You sat through hours, sometimes days, or weeks, in boredom between pure terrors.

He was pleased with the ship, the engines, and his crew's performance.

Trent saw a bright light close to them and used the LMI to check the distance. The LMI revealed the light was stationary, but another object came at them fast. Trent reported it to John. John knew what it was, and ordered George to lock an LDC on the incoming missile.

"Target acquired," George said.

"Take it out."

With precision, the LDC beam struck the object and a massive cloud of space debris and missile parts lit up for several seconds, and then disappeared. They cheered on the flight deck.

"Excellent, now power up the RG and target the bright white light."

George armed the RG. They heard the power surge from the reactor.

"Acquired, Commander."

"Fire Rail Gun."

Everyone on the ship felt the vibration. The RG threw out a dense white blanket of energy between the ship and the ISS. The light speed munitions sped across the vast distance and destroyed the space station. The Russians had tried to kill SEEDS–2025, but failed. Debris from the space station illuminated for a second then disappeared into the black of space.

The crew cheered again.

"Remind me to paint a small ISS on the nose of the ship when we get to Titan," Ricky said.

"I wouldn't celebrate. As soon as the Russian ship finds out, they'll find us, and retaliate. They could take our colony, eradicate us, and have no direct conflict with the Chinese on Mars," John said.

"Do you think so?" Brenda asked.

"I have no doubt, but we will face off with them should they come. They may not want to fight. Don't forget, there's no place for them to go."

The colonist's cabins had a bed, desk with a computer, recreational electronics, no window, and a small combination bathroom/shower.

The common joke among the colonists was the cabins felt like being inside an egg, and the FRMs felt like egg cartons. They spent most of their time in the GR where the spaciousness made up for the cramped quarters.

They volunteered for light duties, and enjoyed the recreation activities. Many spent their time on the Observation Deck looking out the massive portal looking at the wonders of the universe.

They all wanted to visit the flight deck where the crew would explain where they were in the solar system, and see how fast they were traveling on the speed indicator on the forward panel.

The flight deck instrument they liked the most was the countdown clock to destination. It put everything into perspective.

The GLs ran drills to keep emergency procedures fresh in their minds.

The PhD's who had labored hard to make the project a reality, were in their labs on board to continue making incredible discoveries. They already had several modifications for the ship.

Rogers, of Rogersnite fame, worked with flexible composite materials, and experimented with what he called "programmable matter." With an electrical input, he could make the material take the form of whatever he wanted. Rogers didn't know why it worked. He stumbled upon it after trying one of Trent's suggestions for another project he worked on.

Thurgood studied how the ship's circadian lighting affected he colonists.

Winslow was ecstatic Tommy didn't experience any abnormalities. He wired him up to the monitors and couldn't find a single flaw, his other organs were performing better than ever. Tommy did find it difficult to relax and fall asleep.

"Go to the gym, or the G-pool. Swim some laps until you're fatigued enough to fall asleep. Ask Dr. Baker for sleep meds," Winslow said.

If anyone was near when Tommy was in the G-pool, they witnessed his incredible swimming ability. They didn't know why he could swim as fast as he did.

Winslow considered telling Sanders about Tommy's progress at dinner, but he didn't want to seem overly optimistic. The ship was still a long way from Titan. If

Tommy maintained his current health status throughout the entire journey it would, Winslow believed, change the dynamic for any future space flights. For one thing, they could leave the Robonauts back in storage where they belonged.

Prized passenger, Trent Garth, was buried in discoveries, and able to prove a variety of theories believed to be unsolvable for centuries. It was an effort for Fulbright to get him to get him to slow down.

Bryan and Isaac sat in the Conference Room.

"I'm impressed by our researchers. They went right to their labs, and got back to work," Bryan said.

"I spoke with Trent. He told me about a propulsion theory he found buried in Nikolai Tesla's blueprints. One was for a system Tesla called, 'Space Drive,' or the 'Anti-electromagnetic-field-propulsion system.' Tesla believed electromagnetic waves could push and pull space. The Hall Effect applies the theory in semiconductor magnetic sensors called MHD. Tesla also believed in universal gravity, inertia, momentum, and movement of heavenly bodies, including all atomic, and molecular matter. His Dynamic Theory of Gravity collapsed Einstein's theories. The entire universe flows, and whirls, at the speed of light, he believed, so his answer to space travel was to ride the gravitational waves of the universe," Isaac said.

"Nikolai always believed the universe could work for us. Everything we need, like limitless energy, is out there for us to take," Bryan said.

"John."

"Yes, Trent."

"We might see the edge of the "Black Widow" pass."

"The Black Widow?"

"It's a pulsar passing through the galaxy at more than a million miles plus an hour. We're far enough away, so we won't be caught in its shock wave. It would tear the ship apart."

"How can it be moving at a million miles per hour, faster than light? We wouldn't see it."

"You're correct, but if we got too close, we'd *feel* it."

"You're sure we are far enough away from it right?"

"Positive, John."

"I can always throttle back the engines."

"No, we're safe."

John gave Brenda a wide-eyed look.

"It would be an awesome wave to ride," Danny said.

He grew up on Oahu, and was an avid surfer.

"Anything else we should watch for, Trent?" John asked.

"If we were to traverse the Milky Way, and travel too close to the super black hole at the center of the galaxy, we'd encounter the most violent entity in the universe called a *blazar*."

"I used to have one in my closet back home," Ricky said.

"Not a blaze*r*, a *blazar*," Trent said.

Winslow walked onto the flight deck.

"Hello, Trent, how's John treating you?"

"I have no complaints."

"Excellent, Trent. How about you, John, and crew?"

"We're good," Rhian said.

"Good to hear, so far space travel has been agreeable and without incident. Elan has some balls!"

Brenda and Susan turned toward him.

"What? Because I said *balls*?"

Seeing the looks they gave him, he apologized.

"We have strict rules about such remarks on board the ship. Please read your manual, page 74," John said.

"You may have jinxed the flight," Danny said.

"Oh, come on now, there's no such thing as *jinx*."

"What can I do for you, Steven?" John asked.

"Have you a moment to speak alone?"

"Brenda, you have command."

She acknowledged as the two men stepped outside the flight deck door.

"What's up?"

"I wanted to talk to you about Tommy."

"Good, or bad?"

"Excellent, John, even his other organs are in better condition than they were when we left. I suspect space has had a beneficial effect on him. I'm keeping a close eye on him though."

"So am I whenever we're together. Tommy appears to be his usual self. I'm glad to hear the results, and I'm sure Bryan and Isaac will be happy with your report."

"I'll wait on the report. We have a long way to go."

"You mean you don't want to *jinx* your research?"

"Okay, I get it, the crew is superstitious."

John returned to the flight deck.

Michael stood by the digital recorders that captured every utterance from Trent. He observed the flow of ones and zeros from the Earth-famous astrophysicist.

There wasn't anyone on Earth, so now he was famous to only those on the ship. Trent awed Michael by the scope of his accomplishments.

Trent, he recalled, was the reason he wanted to become an astrophysicist.

Isaac walked up to him.

"I wonder what the Chinese and Russian ships have planned now that there's no Earth."

"You can predict what they think. One shot could end it for both. Maybe they can learn to live on Mars in peace. Whatever they do, John and his crew will watch for them," Michael said.

Michael took the opportunity to tell Isaac about his relationship with Alex.

"Old news, Michael."

"How did you know?"

"I recognized the signs."

"Do you approve?"

"Do you need my approval? Be good to my little girl, she makes her own decisions. If she finds you appropriate, so do I."

"Appropriate?"

Bryan, Isaac, and Elan stood on the riser in the GR. Bryan spoke.

"Our home planet died because of the weaknesses of our species. The innocents, and the evil, died in the flames. We felt those flames during our escape to the ship. We were the last survivors as far as we know. As he has done so many times before with SEEDS, Elan saved all our lives. He is a true hero."

Elan's head was down.

"So, what happens now? Today and forever, we will honor their memories, but we must put our focus on the mission. We have more reason now to survive. We carry a precious cargo. The ship has surpassed our expectations. You need to stay healthy. If you have difficulty sleeping, see Dr. Baker. If you're in distress, talk to someone."

He waved his hand toward those standing with him on the riser.

"You still have us, and we are determined to succeed. You'll soon have a new home, a new life, another chance to build a better society. If you have questions, bring them to us, or whenever you see the crew ask them. Until we reach Titan, and the colony is thriving, the five of us will remain in leadership roles. The Commander can override us if an issue affects the ship, and our safety. While en route, we will select a governing body, and write a constitution guided by our constitutional law expert, Dr. Goldman. I encourage every one of you to take an active part in deciding what your government and laws should be."

Time healed heartbreak. Weeks passed as the ship rocketed to Titan. Dr. Britte popped his head into the flight deck.

"John, may I come in?"

"Please, Phillip, it's good to see you. What can I do for you?"

"Well, I didn't want to impose. I saw Steven in the next module, and I'm certain he was a handful."

"Two of my crew are thrilled you're here."

WCS Chan's shift had ended, and WCS Tinsdale replaced him. Both were elated to meet the man who led the department, which created the weapons systems.

"Dr. Hammerstein is right behind me. Can I bring him in?"

"Please."

John made the introductions, and watched as Danny and Ricky shook both doctor's hands, and told them how amazing they were.

"Gentlemen, I didn't design the weapons systems. Dr. Hammerstein here created the Rail Gun's ammunition, and the laser weapons. John, I wanted to know when you would like to test the weapons systems."

"We did."

"I'm sorry, what?"

"Trent alerted us to an incoming missile from the Russian controlled ISS when we passed it leaving Earth. George, there in the chair, took it out with one shot. How often do we need to test the RG system?"

"Once per flight should do," Phillip said.

"RG check is complete as well."

"What do you mean?"

"George also took out the ISS with the RG. The LDCs were impressive, Phillip, but I hope we never have to use them again."

Hammerstein never said a word the entire time he was in the cockpit. John bet Ricky, Hammerstein wouldn't say a word all the way to Titan.

"Hunter, you have command. I'm headed to my cabin after a walk through the ship."

"I have command," Hunter said.

John passed through the airlock and found Clifford dictating notes.

"How are the passengers holding up?"

"I gave out a few Nano's for them to swallow, and told them to call me in the morning," Clifford said.

"Clifford, something's wrong."

"What, John?"

"Everything is fine, too good."

"Where I come from that's a good thing."

"Sure, but we're farther out in space than any human has traveled, and we haven't had one major problem. Even destroying the Russian ISS was effortless. I killed them as if I turned off a light switch."

"Well, we still have a long way to go, twelve months and two weeks, plus establishing the colony. I'm sure you'll come to me complaining about all the problems then. Get some sleep, John, my orders."

"Good idea. Goodnight, Clifford."

"Goodnight, John."

He entered the Cryo Module. He looked in every cryo-bed, and verified the LEDs were green. He was tempted to shake the beds. He looked through the VOE windows, and checked its lights were green.

He passed through the next bulkhead.

Food Service never closed. He ordered a turkey sandwich and a side of potato salad from Sally behind the counter. She typed in his request, and a second later the pre-packaged sandwich was on his tray.

"Commander, something to drink?"

"Water, please."

She took a paper cup and filled it out of the dispenser adding some ice cubes, a coveted item.

"Did you chip the ice from one of the cryo-beds?"

She laughed.

"And how are you, Commander?"

"Good, are you anxious to get to Titan?"

"*Yes*, I'm a Hydroponics Specialist. It's why I work in Food Service. What I feed you here, I follow in my study all the way through filtration, and purification, to the hydroponic racks."

"Sounds like studying an IN & OUT Burger."

"Kind of, is there any chance I can visit the flight deck?"

"Of course, schedule a time with your GL."

"Will she know when WCS Ricky Tinsdale is on duty?"

"Your GL can find the information for you."

"Thank you, Commander, some weapons test we had, huh?"

"It wasn't a test. It was real."

"Did WCS Tinsdale fire the weapons?"

"No, George TwoBears did."

"Awesome!"

John found a table to eat his sandwich. The dining area was large enough to feed fifty colonists at a time. He was hungry, so the sandwich, and potato salad disappeared fast. After he stopped to answer questions from the other diners, John placed his trash in the disposal unit next to the bulkhead.

He stepped through to the next module, and verified the cargo was secure. He continued to the EPM and spoke with the engineers. He visited the GR and stood by the Observation Deck portal to get a renewed perspective on how small man was in the vast universe. He came across a group of doctorates discussing the weapons test and answered their questions. Before he left the GR, he stopped by the animal and fish farms. The two gave off a definite odor, but after standing inside for a while, he got used to it. He spoke with a Noble Prize winner who monitored the animals.

"You seem to enjoy it here. I didn't take you for an outdoorsman," John said.

"At first, I found it disgusting," Wiggins said.

He patted one of the animals.

"After a while, you feel close to them. I've spent most of my life in a lab. I enjoy the change."

"What better way of saving our humanity than keeping a human connection to the animal kingdom."

"I believe so, Commander, I've even named them. So, is the ship on Auto-Titanaut?"

"It's on shift change. I finished my eight hours and was headed for my quarters when I decided to stretch my legs."

"You'll find a happy group. I haven't heard any complaints despite the news about Earth."

"Good to hear."

"Say 'Hello' to Trent for me, would you please."

"Trent never sleeps. He's done a lot of research."

"Trent's been that way since I've known him."

"I should go. I still have a third of the ship I haven't walked through."

"Stop by anytime, Commander."

The fish farm was on Auto-Fish, not much to do but watch them swim in circles inside the large graphene tank. John guessed it might take the two Robonauts, plus ten men like Tommy to transport the tank to the colony.

Beyond the fish farm were the compact versions of the labs with scientists working on their projects. He decided not to disturb them. They were Michael's problem. He was too brain-challenged to withstand an in-depth discussion.

He surveyed the GR.

The colonists looked like they were on a Caribbean cruise and not hurtling through the solar system. A few scientists enjoyed the G-pool. They looked odd in swimsuits after seeing them in white smocks. He waited until more swimmers exited the elevator, one was Susan.

"Hey, John, where're you headed?"

"Back to my quarters to read and get some sleep."

"You should go to the G-pool."

"With that bikini, you better be careful, there are geek sharks in swim trunks there."

"Should have brought my spear gun, huh? Anything new on the flight deck?"

"No, it's quiet. The sound of the fans cooling the instruments will lull you to sleep."

"I decided a few laps would wake me up. Tommy will be there. I don't know how he does it, but that boy can swim."

"I know his secret."

"Tell me."

"Can't, I took an oath."

"No, you didn't."

"Yeah, I'm a 'made' swimmer. I held water in my hands while the Swimfather put a cigarette out in the water.

The elevator doors insisted on closing. John stepped in and waved goodnight to her. When the doors opened on the main ship, inquisitive scientists surrounded him.

"Where are we?"

"Space."

"How much longer, Daddy?"

"Not funny."

"I saw an alien in the quarters next to mine."

"Let's drop the alienophobia. Do keep your eyes and ears open. Look around to find issues before they become problems. I like to catch problems early before they get out of hand," John said.

They agreed. It was John's subtle reminder to them they weren't on a Caribbean cruise.

The crowd dispersed, and John hurried to his cabin where he ruminated about the responsibility resting on his shoulders. His dad was asleep for the night.

John's day was over. He opened his favorite crime fiction writer's last book. C. A. Stone, his favorite author, died in the fire of nuclear war.

Chapter 5

SEEDS–2025 had been en route to Titan for nine months without incident. The crew had to force themselves to practice drills. The SE–15's were superb thrusters. The engineers wondered if the commander planned to test the ANNULAR, and VASIMR.

Winslow lectured Tommy during his physical examination.

"You are not on board the ship to collect as many conquests as you can. You are a *test* case for future travel and colonization. You know the regulations about relationships during travel on the ship. You're a flight officer and should be an example for the others. You won't be one if I have this conversation again, understood?"

"But, Doc, I'm not *romantically* involved with any of them, and the rule book says it's okay."

"Tommy, I'm not asking you to stop. I'm *ordering* you to stop. Don't force me to go to John. He'll put you into one of the cryo-beds and deep freeze you until we get to Titan."

"What do you recommend I do instead?"

"Read a book, go to the gym. Your two hearts have to be in perfect working order when we get to

Titan, so we can prove we don't need Robonauts."

Tommy didn't like being scolded. He also didn't want to have his manhood frozen for the rest of the flight. Most of all, Tommy didn't want to be taken off flight status, so he walked to the eBook library to find a few downloadable books to read. When he was off-duty, he visited Hammerstein to talk about the weapons.

On the flight deck, the "dark duty" shift was the most difficult. No one wanted to work it. The only way to stay alert was to turn up the flight deck and instrument panel lights to simulate daylight. On rare occasions, only one flight officer occupied the flight deck at night for several hours. If you were the person who was there, under those circumstances, you had a propensity to hear strange noises, which magnified until you were uncomfortable.

Lukas found himself in such a situation. For an hour, he heard strange sounds, creaking noises, and people speaking when no one was there. It was a psychological phenomenon known as *pareidolia*. The mind would see, or hear, familiar images, or sounds where there were none, or hear indistinct conversations when a fan turned.

Trent sensed when a crew member experienced pareidolia. He would distract the person by asking a question because he wanted them to know he was there.

"Lukas do you think the universe is a hologram?"

"We have astrophysicists on the ship who believe it."

"But what do you believe? Speculate, it's not a

graded question."

"It could be, but wouldn't it look wavy and transparent like when Princess Leia popped out of R2D2? You're the most brilliant scientist in the universe. You said we existed in a black hole."

"Einstein wasn't right all the time either. Anaxagoras, a Greek philosopher in ancient times, believed the universe was part of a living organism. Plato, also an old man, later formulated the thesis, and called it the 'Organismic Theory.'"

"The Ancients had their own ideas?"

"Yes, they were as curious about how things worked in the universe as we are. They didn't have the tools yet to sturdy such things. Maybe during our journey, we will find the answers to questions from millennia ago."

Lukas's mind wrapped around what Trent said. He forgot about the creaking sounds, and indistinct voices.

Michael rolled over to shut off the alarm clock. He woke Alex with a kiss.

"I don't want to get up!"

"But the sun is about to break the horizon."

"We're in space. One more hour, *please* Michael."

"Of sex?"

"Sleep, Michael, sleep!"

"Okay, one more hour, no, make it two."

"Are you serious, or being sarcastic?"

"Serious. Sleep another hour or two. I'll see you when you get to the Conference Room."

"You're cold, deep space cold. I'll get up."

"I told Isaac we're sleeping together. He said he approved if you did. I asked if I could call him 'Dad.' He stared at me over his reading glasses, and threatened my life."

"You didn't, oh how funny."

Thirty minutes later, Alex and Michael walked into the Conference Room. As usual, Isaac had his nose buried in papers while doing research on his computer.

"You look perplexed, Dad."

"It isn't I can't comprehend the information in front of me. It's the amount of what Trent sends. I have three researchers and Becca sorting through the pile trying to organize it into general categories. Maybe I'll call Fulbright and have him turn off the implant until I catch up."

He never looked up from his work.

"Good morning, you two, have a seat," Bryan said.

His face didn't hide his worries. They still had a long way to go, and a universe of possibilities could go wrong.

After a good night's sleep, John met with John, Sr. for breakfast.

"I can't explain it, but I sleep like a baby in my quarters. I know everyone else hates their eggs," John, Sr. said.

"What do you want to do before my shift?"

"What about the gym? I see a belly popped on you. Too much sitting, John."

They went for breakfast then the gym for a light

workout.

John said goodbye and hugged him. He had his shift to cover.

He sat in the command seat. Brenda was the official captain. Sean performed the FO duties. Edward yawned, and stretched, before accepting the SCNO changeover. WCS Danny waited for Tommy to replace him.

John read the previous crew's report, noted any discrepancies then reviewed the latest updates. He said "Good morning" to Trent and commanded a surprise drill.

"Engine Failure!"

Brenda ran the checklist and commanded a relight of the failed engine. The engine did not re-light.

"Engine Shutdown Checklist," Brenda said.

FO Sean began to read the checklist. Brenda replied to each challenge. When the checklist required a response from the WCS, there was a pause. John looked up. Danny looked at John.

"Did you want me to continue, or do you want to wait for my replacement, Commander?"

"Who's missing?"

"Tommy."

He told Sean to check Tommy's cabin.

"Empty."

John told Sean to page Winslow over the PA. Steven called on the intercom.

"We seem to be missing a crew member on the flight deck, and I hope I don't have to check every egg to find him," John said.

"He's not missing, John. I found him face down in the G-pool. We almost have him out of the water. I'll take him to Medical as soon as the gurney gets here."

"I'll meet you there. Brenda, you have command. Get Simon up here to fill in as captain."

"He worked two shifts," Sean said.

"Sean, if you feel up to it, take the captain's seat. Get Rhian, or Lukas, to cover for you."

John walked out of the flight deck to Medical and waited for Tommy's arrival.

The news of Tommy's death struck him hard, but he couldn't show it.

The gurney arrived at the G-pool with Dr. Baker. He pronounced Tommy dead at the scene.

The gurney, Clifford, and Steven arrived in Medical. They rolled the gurney into the operating theater below the surgical light.

Tommy was covered with a sheet until the hatch to the Medical Station was secured.

"He must have passed away last night after the others retired to their eggs. A few stragglers walked to the Observation Deck, but from there, they couldn't see the G-pool. I walked through after working in my lab and saw Tommy. He had to be in the water a while, that's why he's bloated."

Steven turned to Clifford.

"Tommy was a test case for future flights. He has two hearts. I believed it would give the colonists an edge on Titan."

Clifford got angry.

"I'm not sure what you did was ethical, Steven."

"Clifford, in SEEDS you do know we do research. We try to find ways to make the colonists successful on worlds their bodies aren't accustomed to, so they have a better chance of survival. We can't save humanity if Robonauts are the survivors. Right now, I'd appreciate it if you would do a VA on him, I'll assist. I have to know what failed, my research, or Tommy's behavior."

"How long before you know something, Steven?" John asked.

"The set up for the VA takes an hour. Once it's operational, it'll take a half hour to find out what went wrong. I spoke to him yesterday. I had to tell him to stop having sex with every consenting female on board, or he would lose his flight duties. I'm guess he spent his time working out his sexual energies in the G-pool, but he still should be alive."

"I'll be on the flight deck, When you find out the cause was, call me. Clifford, please check his records for his burial preference, on the planet, or Space Burial."

"Is there family to be notified?"

"No, we were Tommy's only family. I'll make the announcement and hold a service for him later this evening. Steven, please advise Bryan and Isaac about what happened."

He returned to the flight deck and told the crew.

"Tommy drowned in the G-pool last night.

"In the G-pool? He was in excellent shape. I watched him do fifty laps in under four minutes," Brenda said.

"Well, since Tommy's passed, I can tell you, but what I tell you stays with the crew only, understood?"

They agreed.

"Tommy was a SEEDS test case. Winslow implanted a second heart inside him before we left Earth. Bryan, Isaac, and I were the only other ones on the ship who knew. Tommy, Winslow hoped, would be stronger on the planet, and if he succeeded, he could do the same transplant to the other colonists, so they would have better chances of survival. The VA will tell us what went wrong."

"It explains why he slept with two, and three, 'Titanettes' a night," Edward said.

An hour passed. Steven spoke to John on the flight deck about the results of the VA.

"His aorta blew out. Tommy was told to select one heart at a time, unless there was strenuous activity required. He left both hearts beating. In the next procedure, I'll need to reinforce the aorta."

John stared at the esteemed researcher with two Nobel Prizes.

"While you're installing a more rugged aorta, you might want to downsize the libido. Tommy was only twenty-six. What made you believe he'd select only one heart?"

"He was told of the dangers, but chose to take a chance," Steven said.

Baker relayed the news of Tommy's passing to each computer in the colonist quarters, and included the time for the memorial service. On the form all colonists filled out before departure, Tommy had checked the box, "Space Burial."

The recreation room filled with colonists and available crew for the service. Trent watched the monitor on the flight deck. There weren't any flowers. There wasn't a guest book to sign. Tommy lay on the gurney dressed in his uniform. They didn't wrap him like a mummy. Instead, Dr. Baker used a method called "plastination." A solution with plastic hardened his cells, and veins. The crew draped a SEEDS–2025 flag over him with his WCS wings laid on top. John gave the eulogy.

"Weapons Control Specialist Tommy Maxwell will leave on his solitary journey across the universe. He was an excellent flight officer, and contributed to the success of SEEDS beyond the call of duty. He was also my friend. Tommy was alone in his personal life. He had no living relatives when he signed on with SEEDS. We were the only family he had. We will miss his boyish charm, and his desire to be the best. The service is concluded."

John directed Tommy's fellow WCSs to roll the gurney to an airlock of the ship. They transferred his body to a steel table. The airlock was sealed then depressurized. John pressed the hatch release.

The pressure inside the airlock equalized with the vacuum of space.

Mourners chose the Observation Deck portal to watch Tommy's body drift away from the ship and into eternity.

John closed the airlock's hatch.

"Try to remember, Son, it's not about those who left us. It's about those who remain," John, Sr. said.

You couldn't miss the fifth planet from the sun, Jupiter. The planet filled the forward windows of SEEDS–2025. Jupiter was a helium and hydrogen gas giant. NASA probes showed Jupiter spun so fast, its gravity could produce a massive gravitational slingshot for the ship, if Saturn's violent discarding of rocks and dust weren't a factor. John decided to get as close as possible to take whatever Jupiter had to give. A powered slingshot close to Jupiter, would give the ship the greatest delta-V.

"First Officer, plot us on a course around the mass of gas. Trent, see if you can find the edge of Jupiter's infamous gravity, and please include a plot of Jupiter's moons, so we don't collide with any, unless you think this is a bad idea," John said.

"It shouldn't be a problem if the parameters mentioned are adhered to, John."

"The colors of Jupiter are brilliant. Can you imagine what Galileo Galilei, who first discovered the planet, would say if he were here right now," Brenda asked.

"He'd say, 'Did I discover that beautiful planet?'" Sean said.

"The planet rotates every ten hours, so we should be able to get a photo of the Great Red Spot," Brenda said.

"I'm sorry, did you say the Great Wet Spot?" Ricky asked.

John told him the remark was inappropriate.

"The Great Red Spot's winds of greater than 539 KPH swirls the cloud bands," Brenda said.

"That's true, Brenda, very good," Trent said.

"If for some reason we can't land on Titan, Jupiter's moon, Europa, is one of our alternate destinations because there is evidence an ocean lies beneath its icy surface. Sound about right, Trent?"

"Correct, Lukas."

Whenever Trent answered in short sentences, it meant he was deep into an equation, or theory.

"Forget Titan. I say we find Europa on the map and park. I need to stretch my legs," Ricky said.

"You'll have to stretch your legs in the GR. We still have about seven-hundred-fifty million miles to Titan. If this slingshot works, we may cut the distance down to five-hundred-million," Trent said.

"I'm for the slingshot," Sean said.

The first officer plotted the course. Confirmation of the trajectory appeared on the MFC screen, the PFC instrument panels, and Trent's monitor. The colonists were told to harness in their eggs. At first, there was no change in their speed.

"First Officer, check your computa—"

The ship lunged forward, buffeted, and the G-forces forced them deep into their seats.

Looking out the forward windows nothing appeared different, but if you could focus on the speed indicators, they, and the accelerometer confirmed they had caught a slingshot tailwind. The G-forces increased until the crew and colonists had to force themselves to inhale and exhale, as they were taught to do in training. A few colonists screamed inside their eggs.

The crew saw Europa and Io, two of Jupiter's moons in the distance approach fast, but they were in no danger of a conflict.

After the slingshot ended, Brenda reset the heading. They covered a significant distance before the airspeed and accelerometers began to roll back to normal. The crew and colonists relaxed. John waited fifteen minutes before allowing the colonists to leave their eggs.

"That was an impressive maneuver, John," Trent said.

"Can we do it again?" Brenda asked.

John tried to look like he had done it a thousand times.

"Sure, Captain, after the colonists change their jumpsuits," Ricky said."

After they left their eggs, several scientists knocked on the flight deck door. They wanted to ask about the slingshot. They had a thousand questions for John and Trent. They would have to wait until a crew change. They were told to meet with John in the GR in an hour.

John sent Danny to find his dad and bring him to the flight deck. John, Sr. had slept through the slingshot.

"What's everyone so excited about?" he asked.

Alex, Michael, Bryan, Isaac, and Elan wanted to hear about the slingshot maneuver. They waited in the Conference Room. While they waited, Elan took out a pocket flask, unscrewed the cover, and took a drink. He held it out for Isaac who didn't hesitate. Alex caught them and chastised her father for setting a bad example. Michael took the flask followed by Alex.

John entered the Conference Room with Brenda.

"When are you going to run tests on the ANNULAR and VASIMR thrusters?" Bryan asked.

"I'll call engineering right away."

John told Brenda to return to the flight deck and prepare one of the two thrusters for the test. John sat at the conference table.

Brenda entered the flight deck.

"Ready for some more fun?"

"What kind of fun, Brenda?" Trent asked.

"Bryan wants us to run tests on the thrusters."

She picked up the intercom, and told the engineers to advise when they were ready.

"Are we shutting down the SE−15's for the test?" Rhian asked.

"No, the ion propulsion thrusters will take at least a month to produce enough thrust for the ship. If one ion thruster can produce enough thrust to keep the ship at its current speed, we could shut down the SE−15's. It would help to save the methane fuel. We'll see, that's what the test will determine."

An engineer called the flight deck.

"Commander, we have positioned the ANNULAR for the test. We're good to go here."

"Thank you. We'll light it."

"ANNULAR Start Checklist.

The thruster ignited.

"ANNULAR thruster gages are in the green," Rhian said.

"Now we have a month to keep an eye on it. Keep a log of the readings."

Brenda worked the rest of the shift.

John briefed in the Conference Room. John, Sr., found him there and reminded John they had a reservation at the Virtual Golf course.

One month and five days passed. John sat in the command chair mid-shift. Dr. Clemons joined the crew on the flight deck.

"The ANNULAR is producing thrust."

"Shut down one SE-15 to see if we slow, Captain," John said.

He advised engineering of the shutdown. All eyes were on the speed and accelerometer indicators. After SE–1 shut down, they noted there was a slight degradation in speed.

"The ANNULAR is strong," William said.

They waited to see if the speed stabilized. It did.

"William, ready for the shutdown of SE–2, 3?" John asked.

"Yes, please."

"Captain, shut down SE–2 and 3."

The second chemical rocket went silent. Again, all eyes were on the speed and accelerometer indicators. Although there was a slight speed deterioration, the ANNULAR still held a decent speed, and they burned far less methane. They waited another half hour to see if there was a further degradation of speed. None was noted and the ANNULAR increased the ship's speed slightly.

"William, this is incredible, no moving parts and screaming fast," John said.

"True, but remember the SE–15's gave it a chance to get up to speed. The ANNULAR required over a month to produce such results. We should bring Elan to the flight deck to see how its performing," William said.

John sent Hank to retrieve Elan. He found Elan in the EPM leaning over the ANNULAR. They walked onto the flight deck twenty minutes later.

"What do you think about the ANNULAR, Elan?" John asked.

"It burns far less methane, John. Hi, William. An impressive thruster once it gets on up on its hind legs."

"I believe we found a good combination under the circumstances, Elan," William said.

He looked at Elan who looked at John who looked at Elan. They high-fived.

The ANNULAR held roughly ten percent more speed.

"Impressive," William said.

"When should we light the SE-15s?"

"Before we swap out the VASIMR for the ANNULAR," Elan said.

"William, we can stop on our way to the EPM and tell Bryan and Isaac about the ANNULAR."

"Call us after the VASIMR swap," John said.

On their way out, Elan and William were in a

deep discussion about the ion thruster. Both hoped they would have the same results with the VASIMR.

They found Bryan and Isaac huddled in the Conference Room. More papers were strewn over the table. Isaac rubbed his eyes because of the eye strain. Bryan took a bite from his sandwich. They were elated by the news.

"Oh, by my calculations, we saved one month, thirteen days, and four hours of flight time with the slingshot maneuver," Elan said.

"Great work, crew. Every achievement we make is another milestone for SEEDS," John said.

Hunter, Sean, Susan, and Danny entered the flight deck for the crew change.

"Now *you* have all the glory, John," Hunter said.

"There's no glory on this ship for individuals, unless you're Trent. For us, it's a shared glory. We're a team. We rely on each other, and we still have a long way to go. We speak with one voice," John said.

His words were a reminder and not a reprimand.

"John, I never get a chance to harass you."

"Hunter, we're running the ANNULAR only. Keep an eye on the speed, if it decays, engage the −15's. You may hear from Elan if he's ready to swap out the ANNULAR for the VASIMR. If he is, light the −15's."

They heard a soft knock on the door. Hunter opened it and Phillip asked to come in.

"Make room for the doctor," John said.

"Several of my colleagues promise not to disrupt your work, but they'd like to ask some questions about the ion thruster."

John looked at Hunter.

"Are you okay with answering questions for them?"

Hunter leaned next to John's ear.

"And tell them what? We weren't here."

"Talk to them as if you were, systems are systems. What's the problem? *You* get the glory."

"Got it."

"Dr. Britte, please tell your colleagues they are welcome to come in, but two at a time, please," Hunter said.

"Excellent, Commander."

Britte left the flight deck.

Before John left, he made sure everyone was up to speed on the latest information about the thruster.

He was tired, and needed to close his eyes in the solitude of his cabin, but he promised his dad they'd see a movie. John, Sr. told him about the new friends he made in the GR.

Brenda went to the GR to answer questions.

Sean stopped in Food Service.

Edward went to his cabin to relax with Marley.

During John's shift the next morning, inside the cargo module, Robonaut activated. Its eyes opened, and its head turned from side-to-side. The Transhuman dismounted from its storage rack, and made its way to the GR elevator. No one was near to notice. As the double doors of the elevator opened, screams were heard. Several colonists backed away from it. The Robonaut proceeded to the Observation Deck and stopped.

Rhian called John and said an emergency was in progress in the GR. John arrived six minutes later and saw Robonaut was loose. The Observation Deck was jammed full of Titanauts. John took a position in front of the robot, and searched for its OVERRIDE switch.

John told one of the GLs to tell Sanders to come to the Observation Deck.

John evaluated the situation.

Is it uncontrollable? Is it dangerous? How do I stop it? Where's the OVERRIDE switch?

He knew there was no way he could overpower it. The Transhuman stood as still as a statue until its eyes opened, and it began to sing with an electronic voice. The Robonaut struggled with the letter "B."

"Happy Irthday to you, Happy Irthday to you, Happy Irthday, dear Commander, Happy Irthday to you!"

The colonists sang along, and laughed. They ran forward and encircled John. Two GLs carried a cake with candles burning. John was embarrassed, but relieved he didn't have to fight the Robonaut.

A broad smile appeared on his face.

"Whoever set this up will be dropped off *alone* on the next moon."

He made a wish about his dad and blew out the candles. He cut the first piece of cake. John searched the Observation Deck for the mastermind. He saw

Robert leaning against a bulkhead with a smug smile. He mouthed the words "Happy Birthday" to John, and then sent the Robonaut back to its charging station.

"You could have caused a panic."

"How? You were the only one who didn't know it was a prank."

"A good one. You have no idea how many scenarios I ran through to try and stop it."

They ate birthday cake. John made sure someone took slices of the cake to Trent, and the crew. John, Sr. laughed every time he looked at his son.

That afternoon, per the automated circadian clock, the colonists met with Bryan, Isaac, Elan, and Michael for a serious discussion about the rule of law on Titan.

Bryan said they would hold an election for the Colonial Representative who would take control after the colony was established. He asked if anyone wanted to nominate someone.

Two hands rose.

Both men stood to make a statement before the vote.

"I'm Dr. Phillip Britte. I've been with the SEEDS family since the founders asked me to come on board early in the program. I've pledged my knowledge, and my life to SEEDS. Here we are on our way to construct a new home for humanity. It's what I do. I build things, so it makes sense I would offer to help build a safe new world."

Smiles spread across colonist's faces.

"Dr. Winslow, you had your hand up, please say a few words," Bryan said.

Winslow stood.

"I'm Dr. Steven Winslow. I came on board about mid-point. My specialty is biotechnology. I was the surgeon who placed the second heart in Tommy Maxwell. We're not sure if I should try again, so what do I offer you? Right now, my undivided attention toward the governance of the colony. Thank you."

Some heads bobbed.

Dr. Goldman explained the Representative would be the administrator only, and not the lawmaker.

"Every colonist will be provided with a means to vote no matter what the subject, or the law as a democracy should work. Each member of the colony shares in the responsibilities of governance. We do not want to make the same mistakes they made on Earth. When more colonies are established, they will be united as a republic. The SEEDS flag, planted on Titan, will remain the flag of the republic unless otherwise decided by *you*."

After collecting the ballots, the new Representative was named, Dr. Phillip Britte. It was a close vote, so they decided to add Dr. Steven Winslow as Vice-Representative. Both men rose and shook hands. The record showed Britte and Winslow were the first Titanauts chosen to lead the colony.

Michael huffed as if he had run the hundred-yard dash. Alex wanted more, but Michael said contingent on if there was an oxygen bottle nearby. They heard a knock.

"Hey, Bryan, what's up?"

Bryan knew what was *up*.

"I know you took a personal day to get some well-deserved rest, Michael, but I wanted to tell you there's a meeting in an hour in the Conference Room to discuss the ANNULAR and VASIMR's performance."

"I'll get dressed and see you there."

Both Alex and Michael attended the meeting.

"They don't look like much, but they save tons of methane. The only problem with them is they operate at one speed, so when we get closer to Titan, we'll try to coast to slow down, otherwise we'll use the maneuvering SE-15s," Elan said.

"The best of both worlds," Michael said.

"That's what Phillip said that day on Level 7, remember?" Elan asked.

"Sure do."

"I don't know if you heard, Michael, but the colonists voted. Phillip was elected Representative, and Steven Vice Representative," Bryan said.

"All because Elan reminded us we hadn't paid attention to anything other than science," Alex said.

"Phillip and I are headed back to EPM to check on the VASIMR," Elan said.

Outside the conference room, Michael corralled Elan.

"How are you, Elan?"

"Good, why?"

"You work a lot."

"Are you saying that because of what happened to my people? You know everything we do in SEEDS requires a bit of emotional distance, otherwise, we can't move forward. We have a solemn responsibility to get to Titan safe. Being out here in the solar system is dangerous. The universe is unforgiving, Michael."

"We will succeed because we have Bryan, Isaac, and you."

"And we have Alex, and you. I apologize, but I need to go. Phillip and I need to be in the EPM."

Elan walked away with Phillip. Alex studied Elan.

"He's hurting, holding it in. It *will* spill out," Alex said.

"If he's not able to let it out, we may lose a good friend. I need to spend time with him, get him to talk."

"I wouldn't wait too long."

John and John, Sr. walked up.

"Did you hear what Sander's did to me with his Robonaut?"

"What?" Alex asked.

John, Sr. laughed while he told them the story. Alex was hysterical. The four of them decided to see the movie, *Alien*.

After the movie, Michael caught Elan on his way back from EPM.

"When was the last time you got some sleep?"

"What week is this?"

"You need to take a break. I can't afford to lose you. I don't need you sleepwalking out here. I need you. If you break, SEEDS is out of business."

"I can't sleep. I try, but all I do is toss and turn. I read, and toss the book back on the table. I go to the gym, press the weights one time, wipe my sweat, and leave. I feel if I sleep something could go wrong, and I won't be there to fix it."

Elan looked hard at Michael.

"I failed to save even one of them, Michael."

"It wasn't your fault. We lost people too. We won't forget them, but we need to focus on survival now, it's critical."

"I know, Michael, but if I don't work I will come apart. I manage the loss by working."

"What I need is a well-rested superior intellect like yours. Too many mistakes happen when we don't sleep, or have an overwhelming issue to deal with, either one, and the whole thing could come apart. I want you to take time off beginning now, and I want you to see Dr. Baker. He'll give you something to help you sleep."

"I can't. I have the—"

"If you refuse, I'll take it to Bryan and Isaac."

Elan studied Michael's eyes.

"I will, as soon as—"

"Now, Elan."

"Who do you think you are, Michael? If I say I have things to do, I will do them, and you can't stop me."

"Last chance, Elan."

"No."

"Yes."

Elan heard Bryan's voice behind him. He turned.

"If Michael says you need to get sleep, you will sleep. There is no way Michael, or I, will allow you to jeopardize the mission, Elan."

He heard a third voice.

"Neither will I," Isaac said.

Elan saw Clifford behind Isaac.

"Four against one. I'll go with Clifford."

"I'll give you something to sleep, Elan. It's that simple. The ship, the crew, and engineering can do without you for the next twenty-four hours."

"I'll sleep that long?"

"No, but you will sleep, and rest of the time will be under my supervision."

Elan's adrenaline dissipated, the pain burned his neck muscles. He rubbed at them. Clifford walked with him to his quarters, and gave him a powerful sedative. He watched Elan's lights go out.

When Elan woke, he was groggy, and disorientated. The figures in front of him came into focus.

"How do you feel now?" Michael asked.

Elan struggled to focus.

"Here, I have bottles of water for you. Clifford said you'd be dehydrated," Alex said.

Elan squinted at them.

"How long?"

"Thirteen hours."

"Take it slow with the water," Alex said.

Elan took sips from the bottle. When it was empty, Alex handed him another.

"We're still friends, right?"

"Of course, I wouldn't have pushed as hard if you weren't my friend," Michael said.

"Take your time getting up. You're still on mandatory rest time," Alex said.

"You do know before I met you, I was the boss."

"We all were, but we surrendered being the boss to be part of SEEDS. The mission is bigger than us."

Elan swung his legs over to stand.

"Take a steaming shower, eat a huge breakfast, lounge in a chair, and stare out of the Observation Deck portal at the breathtaking universe. Think about all the friends you have who love you," Alex said.

Cary Allen Stone

Chapter 6

"The VASIMR auto-shutdown," Hunter said.

The ship was powered by the thruster since it passed its tests three months prior. Saturn, about the size of a quarter, floated in the ink of space.

"Commander, Engineering, we're on it."

"We'll try a relight, standby," Brenda said.

Brenda sat in the command chair. Hunter in the captain seat, and Rhian was the first officer. Susan scanned indicators for irregularities.

"VASIMR Failure Checklist," Hunter said.

Rhian read the checklist, and Hunter replied then he attempted to relight the thruster.

"Engineering, we were unable to light the thruster. Any suggestions?" Brenda asked.

"Give us a second, Commander."

They waited about three minutes before Engineering called.

"No luck here, Commander, we should try a relight from the BCS."

"Good idea, we might have an issue up here. Captain Ragsdale is on his way."

Brenda moved to the captain's seat. Hunter moved quickly to the BCS. After he completed the checklist, he tried to relight the thruster. It didn't relight. The speed indicator wound down fast.

"Commander, no go on the relight," Hunter said.

"Rhian read the Before Engine Start Checklist." Brenda said.

She engaged all three SE–15's.

The ship drifted forward by momentum, but off course while they worked on the VASIMR.

Brenda entered a new heading into the MFC. Elan and William arrived on the flight deck. Brenda briefed them.

Elan's analytical mind ran through possible scenarios, which could cause the thruster to fail. The ion thruster was simplicity, straightforward in its operation, no moving parts.

"We'll give you a report when we know something. Let's look, William."

They walked briskly to the EPM. By the time they got there, Engineering had run various computer diagnostic programs to see if they missed something in the original design. The engineers had no answers. They were relieved the thruster detected a problem, and auto-shutdown. A catastrophic failure could have damaged the ship.

John slept soundly throughout the night and was refreshed. He heard Brenda's PA to come to the flight deck. He walked through the flight deck's bulkhead door ten minutes later.

"What's up?"

Brenda turned in the command chair.

"The VASIMR auto-shutdown. We don't know why. Engineering tried to isolate the reason. We tried a relight from the flight deck, and the BCS, no go. Elan and William are in EPM."

"Okay, we're back on the SE—15's, so we wait until the engineers figure out the problem. We don't need the VASIMR," John said.

An hour passed, Elan gave an update.

"No answer yet. We can't determine a reason for the auto-shutdown."

"Advise if there's changes," Brenda said.

John looked out the forward windows at Saturn in the distance. The rings were visible and stunning.

"Look for anything out of the ordinary on the instrument panels. Check your readings for the past four hours. There must be some indication, however small, of the impending shutdown. Any ideas, Trent?"

"I don't have an answer for you, Commander."

Elan and William studied the schematics.

"It doesn't make sense," William said.

"No, it sure doesn't," Elan said.

"It's a good thing we have your SE—15's."

"Sometimes new designs have hidden bugs in them."

At the conference table, they listened while Brenda explained the chain of events. The engineers told them what they knew. The computers didn't have answers.

"What we have is dead weight in the EPM. Can we kick it overboard?" Bryan asked.

Glances went around the table.

John, Sr. spoke to John outside the room.

"I think I'll take a nap. I feel a little drained.

"Okay, Dad, let's get a sandwich from Food

Service when you wake up."

"Sounds good, John."

John, Sr. walked toward the elevator. Before he went in, he turned to John.

"I love you, John."

"I love you, Dad."

He entered the elevator and walked to his quarters. He planned to see Dr. Baker after his nap.

Michael went to get some papers in his quarters. As he passed John, Sr.'s egg, he heard a groan. Michael knocked and called out. He twisted the door handle. The door opened, and Michael saw John, SR. clutch at his heart. He tried to revive him, but was unsuccessful. He picked up the intercom and called Dr. Baker. On the table inside, Michael saw a photo of John in his uniform when he graduated from the Academy. Dr. Baker spoke to John outside the Conference Room.

John's guarded command persona broke down when he heard the words. Later in the circadian evening, John struggled with the eulogy.

"We knew how dangerous this journey was. We knew there would be setbacks, 'Potholes in the road' as Dr. Talbot always said. We bury ourselves in our work, although we have the best view of our solar system. I lost my best friend today. I loved John Kelly, Sr. with all my heart, and felt blessed to spend his last days on the ship with him. Goodbye, Dad, I love you."

Like Tommy Maxwell, John Kelly, Sr. was plastinated and sent adrift through the universe. John watched from the Observation Deck portal. He received condolences from the colonists who told stories about his dad, how he used to make them laugh. John thanked Michael for bringing his dad along for the flight.

I'll miss you, Dad.

"I'm certain there are millions of things we didn't consider, but look what happened to Mother Earth. We tell ourselves we're intelligent beings, and able to conquer new worlds. The truth is we're mere children in the universe," Michael said.

Dr. Baker called each colonist, including Michael, to the Medical Station under the guise of regular check-ups. The real reason was he evaluated their states of mind. A few tempers flared on occasion, far less than supernovas in the universe.

"Does that mean we should surrender, and not explore?" Clifford asked.

"No, that's not where I was headed with this. I saw Elan's distress. He believes, if we put our minds to it, we can conquer any problem, but we can't. It's my realization we're not superhuman."

"Should we surrender to Sanders' Robonauts?"

Clifford pressed his stethoscope against Michael's chest and back.

"We could have put our energy into *repairing* the damage humans did to the Earth, and we wouldn't be out here facing the unknown dangers of a chaotic universe."

"Are you sleeping well? Any feelings of anxiety?"

"I sleep well. Anxiety, sure."

"Want a prescription for some pills?"

"The blue ones?"

"No, anxiety pills."

Clifford did all he could to maintain his professional bedside manner.

Hunter was in command. Lukas sat shotgun. Edward monitored systems. WCS Ricky was at station.

"This is Commander Kelly, all crew members, not on duty, report to the Conference Room at 14:00."

They walked to the Conference Room where Bryan, Isaac, Elan, Michael, and Alex waited.

"What's up, John?" Brenda asked.

"We want to discuss the arrival to Saturn," Isaac said.

They took seats around the table.

"We are close to Titan. Elan says we need to slow. Bob programmed the MFC to enter geosynchronous orbit over Base Crater. The maneuvering SE-15s are in the forward position. We've done the approach a thousand times in the simulator," John said.

He drew the arrival on the dry erase board, and explained in detail what would happen, and when.

"The crew will monitor the Auto-Flight system during the approach, prepared to disconnect the Auto-Flight if there are any deviations. Call out anything abnormal."

"What about the colonists?" Brenda asked.

"When we are in a critical phase, they will be harnessed inside their eggs, no exceptions. They will want to know what's happening on the flight deck, so the week before we initiate the approach, we will brief them. Before descent, the flight deck goes sterile. No one will be allowed in or out, and no communications will be made, unless there's an emergency management can't handle. If something is not right, the captain will break off the approach," John said.

"Who's flying the approach?" Hunter asked.

"You are."

Hunter was surprised John gave him the critical assignment. He paid more attention to every word John said.

"In orbit around Titan, we won't be able to see a thing because of the moon's dense atmosphere. What we have now, which we didn't have before, is Elan's Shuttle. He will be descending in the Shuttle down to the surface to evaluate Base Crater. After he returns to the ship, we will have another discussion about sending down the FRMs, and decide if we'll land SEEDS-2025 inside Base Crater."

"We've traveled to Titan for over a year, but now it feels like the year went by fast," Rhian said.

"Did we ever decide what to do if aliens show up?" Ricky asked.

Bryan laughed.

"I want all of you to get plenty of rest. One small mistake can grow into a major disaster fast. Questions?"

None. They looked at the crew on the flight deck on the monitor.

"Questions from the on-duty crew?"

"No, John, we're good."

"Trent?"

"I want to say we've worked toward this for a long time. A successful approach, and landing in Base Crater is another giant step. I watched the crew perform all this time, and I can affirm their dedication is exemplary, and their abilities under all conditions are boundless. I'm proud to be a part of the adventure, and a member of the crew."

"Thank you, Trent, well said."

Bryan and Isaac reviewed the planned procedures at length and were satisfied, so they had no questions.

"Okay, let's get back to work," John said.

He spoke to Brenda about Hunter on their way back to the flight deck.

"His confidence level reached Alpha Centauri."

"Speaking of confidence levels, now all you have to do is fly the ship free from the GR without damaging the ship, and land our kilometer-long SEEDS-2025 on Titan."

"I've studied the separation and landing from every perspective possible. I ran simulations on the computer. I've gone over both procedures in my head since we left Earth. I'm as prepared as I can be. All that's left is doing them."

The week after the discussion about the arrival to Titan, Brenda sat in the command chair.

"Captain, light the maneuvering SE-15s, and shut down the aft SE–15's."

Once the thrusters produced thrust, she executed the step-down to align for the approach.

Three circadian days later, John watched Hunter enter orbit around the moon.

Hunter adjusted the orbit over Base Crater.

Bob's navigational program in the MFC worked perfect.

"Well done, Commander."

"I can see Saturn," Sean said.

"It's that big round ball with the circles around it, right?" Ricky asked.

"I've been looking at it too," Trent said.

Saturn filled the forward windows. The planet was nine times the size of Earth.

Hydrogen and liquid helium were abundant on Saturn, if you could find a way to maneuver the ship in the 1,800 KPH winds to retrieve it.

Trent and the crew observed Saturn's outer moons, Pandora, and Prometheus, both herded the other sixty moons in the rings to keep them from escaping farther into space.

"We have a lock on Base Crater, Commander," Lukas said.

The ship maintained 2100 KM's AGL.

The week before the final approach, Brenda explained the critical maneuvers the crew would use to take the ship into orbit, drop the FRMs, separate from the GR, and possibly land the ship on Titan.

Michael and Elan stood in the back.

"Dr. Mason, when prepared, will descend to the surface inside the Shuttle. Titan's atmosphere is thick and the visibility is restricted. Once Dr. Mason

111

confirms the landing area is acceptable, we will begin separation of the FRMs from the main ship. Each will Autoland inside Base Crater in a circular arrangement, thanks to Dr. Hinkle who programmed them," Brenda said.

She looked at the faces in the room. She held everyone's attention.

"Before we're a go for the FRM drops, you will transfer to the main ship. It will be tight and uncomfortable due to too many bodies in a limited area. You will not be able to harness in, all you will be able to do is brace. Before SEEDS-2025 can set down on the surface, the most critical maneuver of our entire journey will occur, the separation of the ship from the GR. The ship and all Titanauts will be in great danger. If any of the massive GR struts contacts the ship, the damage will be so severe, none of us will survive. Flying the ship out of the GR is a life or death maneuver. If the separation is successful, we will construct the colony."

"What if Elan says we can't land the ship on Titan, or for some reason Commander Kelly chooses *not* to separate from the GR?" William asked.

"Then we remain on the ship until you, Phillip, construct a space elevator to the moon. We could send the cargo, labs, fish farm, animals, the Cryo's and VOEs, and everything else down to the surface on the elevator."

Phillip considered what he had to do to construct the space elevator.

"In either case, the Robonauts will secure the FRMs together, build the dome, and deliver the cargo. After the engineers approve habitation of the structures, Dr. Britte will lead you to your new home. You will help a great deal by not distracting the crew from what they must concentrate on."

"It will be difficult to feel helpless, Captain," a colonist said.

"I understand what you're saying because I always want my hands on the controls, but instead of feeling helpless, feel confident in the crew who brought you to Titan."

"We do have complete trust in the crew," another colonist said.

"So you are not totally in the dark about what is happening and when, I will ask Dr. Hinkle to install monitors throughout the ship, and to put a camera on the flight deck."

Hinkle grunted.

So they can watch either the GR struts tear apart the ship, or the ship impact the surface.

Brenda received a scientist's standing ovation. PhD's never hooped and hollered, but they did applaud with vigor.

Michael and Elan were pleased with Brenda's presentation.

"How did I do?"

"You convinced *me* everything is under control," Elan said.

Alex walked up to them.

"Hungry?"

"Starving," Brenda said.

"That's two of us," Michael said.

"My stomach has been growling," Elan said.

They took the elevator down to Food Service.

Bryan and Isaac were at work back in the Conference Room, papers scattered across the table.

"Isaac, we're almost there," Bryan said.

"When the warheads hit, I was certain we'd be two more charred corpses on the pile."

"You have been a revered collaborator all these years. Look where we took SEEDS. We're about to land the ship on Titan."

"It's a sad accomplishment in a way."

"Why do you say that?"

"You know we did it. The colonists know we did it, but billions of dead don't know."

"The billions who come after us will know, like those who knew what the Founding Fathers did."

They contacted Trent.

"What did you discover today?" Isaac asked.

"I learned, listening to Brenda's briefing, my work on Earth brought me fame, but this point in time is my true purpose in life."

The scientists who devoted their lives to saving humanity, became reflective. Trent was right, their lives were defined by the moment they were in.

The Conference Room door opened. Alex, Michael, and Elan walked in.

"Are you prepared for what comes next?" Elan asked.

A voice from the flight deck answered.

"Yes, Elan, the three of us are prepared."

"Hello, Trent, how's my second favorite scientist?" Alex asked.

Both Isaac and Michael believed they were her first.

"All we must do now is the GR separation. If all goes as planned, we can have our mail sent to Titan," Alex said.

"I love Alex," Bryan said.

"I've loved her all my life," Isaac said.

"Come on, Dad, let's take a walk around the GR, you and me."

Isaac held out his arm for her to take. He was as proud of her as any father would be. They went to observe the universe from the Observation Deck portal.

"What's on your mind, Michael?" Bryan asked.

"Thinking about all the things that could go wrong like I always do, what else?"

On the flight deck.

"Has anyone seen the manual on how to separate

from the Gravity Ring?" John asked.

"Look in the magazine rack in the bathroom, Commander," Ricky said.

Hunter entered the flight deck.

"You lined the ship up perfect for the separation and descent, great job, Hunter."

"Thanks, John, you're either a confidence builder, or a gambler."

"Crew, are you ready for today?"

Elan sat in the Shuttle and waited to coordinate with the flight deck. He would be the first human on the moon, though he wouldn't set foot on it. He didn't like the fact a Robonaut would take the honor.

"Trent?"

"Yes, John."

"How do we look for the drop?"

"We have sixteen days of daylight on Titan to descend the FRMs and ship, so there's no rush. We are a go."

"I complained about working twelve-hour days on Earth, now a half day is *seven* Earth days!" Ricky said.

"Trent, ask Elan if he's ready."

"He said he's wondering what the *blank* you're waiting for."

"Getting my head right."

"John?"

"Yes, Trent."

"I had an idea about the separation. We could have spacewalkers monitor the struts."

"Excellent idea. We'll present it to Bryan and Isaac after we get Elan down to the surface and back."

"Elan, Trent, do you copy?"

"Go ahead, Trent."

"The commander is ready."

Danny turned to John.

"I want to volunteer to be a spacewalker."

"Are you sure?"

"100%. I always wanted to feel what the astronauts did when they went outside the Space Shuttle."

"We haven't even talked to management about it."

"Doesn't matter, put me on the list, please."

"Okay, consider yourself placed on the list we don't have. Let's read the 'Drop the Shuttle Checklist.'"

"We don't have one."

"Make one up. Check all the panels for red annunciators, and things like that," John said.

Brenda entered the flight deck.

"Come to watch, or come to do?" John asked.

"Do?"

He stood up.

"Get in the chair. I'll observe."

She would have asked if he was sure, but he always was, so she took the chair.

The crew did as John ordered and scanned every panel and monitor. They verified Elan would have a safe drop.

Lukas sat as the first officer and watched the systems panels.

George remained on high alert in the event one of Ricky's aliens showed up.

John nudged Brenda.

"Call Elan, Trent, and tell him we are a go for the drop," Brenda said.

"Elan, the Commander says you are a go."

Elan was anxious to land the Shuttle on Titan.

Lukas pressed the release switch and sent the Shuttle on its way

The thrusters orientated its position, and the Auto-land system took the Shuttle down through the thick cloud cover.

Elan watched out the forward windows.

As he descended, he read off his altitude above the ground from the GPR. Trent backed up the GPR altitude with the LMI. Both were within a centimeter of each other.

Elan felt buffeting on the way down.

At nine hundred KMs AGL, the shuttle broke out of the clouds, and a man in a spaceship was the first to see the surface of Titan.

The Auto-Land system counted down over the Shuttle's speaker.

"Fifty...thirty...twenty...ten...five...one."

The Shuttle touched down on Titan.

Elan twisted to see the terrain. He noted the terrain of Base Crater was level and flat.

"I'm on the surface."

Trent repeated the momentous event to the crew.

They celebrated.

Elan studied the tall, jagged precipices around Base Crater The tallest appeared to be about seven-hundred KMs in elevation, about two-hundred-fifty KMs below the cloud cover.

Elan opened the Shuttle's hatch, put one foot on the surface, and closed the hatch fast.

"Elan, what do you see?" Trent asked.

"I see home."

His reply went straight into the new history books. John nudged Brenda again.

"Return the Shuttle."

Elan was disappointed. He wanted to stay longer.

After the Shuttle returned they went back to the Conference Room where Bryan, Isaac, Alex, Michael,

James, Robert, Steven, Phillip, Bob, William, and John sat.

Trent watched on his monitor.

"Why don't you brief us, Elan," Bryan said.

"I encountered light turbulence through the clouds, otherwise, it was a smooth ride. The clouds are thick, no breaks between them, and more cumulus than layered. I broke out at nine-hundred-sixty feet, and it was solid haze until touchdown, but not enough you couldn't see obstructions, sort of like if you wore yellow-tinted glasses. The surface is relatively smooth, good enough to land on, whether it be the FRMs, or the ship. There's more than enough space inside the crater to land several ships. The terrain around Base Crater is, *otherworldly*. For the record, tell Ricky, I didn't see one alien yet."

Everyone in the room let out an uneasy laugh. Elan looked at John.

"If we take it slow, I don't see a problem sending down the FRMs, and landing the ship. The more serious problem is the separation from the GR. The chances of one of those massive struts tearing a gaping hole are high. John, you are a capable aviator, but there are mitigating circumstances not programmed into the flight computers. If you sneeze, we could lose our lives," Elan said.

John showed no emotion and remained silent.

"The ship's fuselage is constructed of composite materials, honeycomb carbon web, and the Rogersnite. It would take a sizable force to smash through the hull," Phillip said.

"Even a tear would be enough to destroy the ship, Phillip. We lose the hull, and we'll die when the ship depressurizes. If there is a power interruption, or failure, we're dead."

"Even with my program in the Auto-flight system and MFC?" Bob asked.

"I'm sure the program is accurate, Bob, but it does not take into consideration high winds, plus any deviation in the maneuvering engine's thrust output could jolt the ship just enough to contact the struts." Elan said.

"I suggested to John we have four spacewalkers at each strut to observe, and report. They could see the distance to the end of the ship," Trent said.

"Regarding the thrust, the SE-15s will remain at idle power, which will be enough to move forward," William said.

"You put four crew members at great risk. How fast can they communicate the changes?" Elan asked.

"John will have the accuracy of Bob's MFC program, but all points are well taken," Isaac said.

"Elan, William, and Trent present strong arguments. Do we proceed with the separation, or go with the space elevator?" Bryan asked.

"The FRMs will have no problem getting to the surface," Bob said.

"The space elevator will delay colonization by six months to a year. We won't have the provisions to keep the colonists fed that long," Phillip said.

"It would be better to get the ship on the planet to offload," Michael said.

"So, what's the best course of action to get the ship free of the GR?" Isaac asked.

"You forget one factor," Robert said.

"What did we miss?" Elan asked.

"Human error, *pilot* error, to be exact, the reason for all aviation accidents on Earth."

John sensed the looks.

"Those errors were because pilots relied on bad information," John said.

"No, John, human input to the computers caused the misinformation, which caused a link in the safety chain to break," Robert said.

"What are you suggesting, Robert, what factor are we missing?" Elan asked.

"My Robonaut should fly the ship out of the GR."

"Not a chance," Elan said.

"How do we know the information programmed into your robot is superior?" John asked.

"Robonaut is not *programmed*. The Robonaut has a microchip with human engrams pressed into it, from a human brain, *my* brain."

Robert clasped his hands together.

"The answer, gentlemen, is in the cargo bay."

"No, not the Robonaut," Elan said.

"Why not? The Robonaut is precise, has human intelligence, and inherent situational awareness at a much faster rate than a man. How about someone on the flight deck accidently tripping into John? And, Elan, isn't the Shuttle autonomous?"

"I wouldn't let the Shuttle fly the ship out of the GR."

"A lot of trust to give a machine stored for a year, Robert," Michael said.

"The maneuver is too critical for us to put all our trust into a computer chip. We discussed how programming could have errors," Elan said.

"The Robonaut doesn't need programming. It's a combination of machine and man, precision and perfection."

"Your argument is, if I rely on the MFCs, which are redundant and not one microchip, everything should be fine. And for the record, I sat on the flight deck for over a year, and not one of my crew tripped."

"Now is not the time to grandstand your robot, Robert," Elan said.

"I'm not grandstanding. I know you're afraid of the future, you, and others, but a future that includes Transhumans is inevitable as it was on earth. The machine made man obsolete. A man cannot do the work of a machine, but a machine can do what a man can do, better and longer."

"Machines led to the destruction of humanity on earth, it's why we're here," Elan said.

"You need not fear the Transhuman. It is the next logical step in human evolution. You will no longer be a *species* which becomes extinct. Your mind is yours, inside a body, or a vessel."

"What happens when the Transhuman decides a mind in a body is a hindrance, desires to destroy it to have more of its own kind?" Michael asked.

"Because it has a *human* mind, and not a programmable hard drive. I'm surprised as scientists you fear the future."

"Robert, my dear friend Albert was afraid of how his work would be applied. As we have seen he was right to be concerned, because his work was used to create weapons of mass destruction. We are the only survivors of billions of humans" Isaac said.

"Our focus should be on the survival of this colony, not unprovable conjectures," Bryan said.

"John, when you flew aircraft on Earth, did you use the autopilot coupled for a Cat IIIA approach?" Robert asked.

"Yes."

"Did you trust the machine to land safely by itself?"

"Yes."

"My Transhuman is the only answer."

"We can argue all day, but let's resolve this discussion by a vote," Bryan said.

They would choose between a man and a machine. John didn't show his feelings, but inside he burned.

"Those in favor of the Transhuman flying the ship out of the GR?"

Bryan, Isaac, James, Bob, William, and Robert raised their hands.

"Opposed?"

Steven, Phillip, Alex, Elan, and Trent on the monitor, raised their hands.

"John, you didn't vote," Bryan said.

"I can do the maneuver. It's up to you to believe in me."

"By majority vote then, the Transhuman will fly

the ship," Bryan said.

He looked at John.

"You do know, John, the vote was a practical one, and not a personal one. We all know and respect you as a skilled aviator who brought us all the way to Titan. I believe your answer to Robert's question about the commercial airline auto-land system pushed the vote in his favor," Bryan said.

They knew John was hurt. He was surprised Bryan and Isaac voted against him. He would see the mission was carried out.

"Robert, John will brief the Robonaut."

"The Robonaut already knows every detail about the ship and its avionics. All the Robonaut needs is to be told to do the task. Do you have a time in mind, Commander?"

"The colonists will be relocated to the GR early in the morning. Once the FRMs are on the surface, we will proceed with the separation. Have *it* on the flight deck an hour before separation."

"Robonaut will be there, John, and the Transhuman is not a robot."

"Michael, please brief us on what happens after the FRMs are down, and the separation from the GR is complete," Isaac said

He ran through the items.

"After the ship is on Titan, the Robonauts will secure the FRMs together in a circle. After, they will construct the dome, and then the exterior facilities for the compact fission reactor, water storage tanks, filtration, and purification systems, and the 10-D workshop. After the engineers have inspected, and determined the colony can support human life, habitation by the colonists will be next. The Robonauts will be unpowered and return to stasis until needed."

"Thank you, Michael. We have a great deal of work to do. Before the structure takes in the Titanauts, Isaac and I will hold a small ceremony at the entrance to plant the SEEDS flag. Phillip and Steven, as the chosen representatives, will then lead the Titanauts into their new home. I recommend you all curl up inside your eggs and get some sleep. Tomorrow will be a very long day for all of us," Bryan said.

Elan, Alex, and Michael walked out together, and waited for John. He left the Conference Room hoping all the others had gone to their quarters.

"I don't know what to say," Michael said.

"Nothing to say."

Robert walked up to John after saying goodnight to some of the others. John held back what he wanted to say to him.

"John, I hope there are no hard feelings. It wasn't my intention to *demote* you. I did intend to *promote* my Robonaut."

"Don't be late. I'll bring my knowledge and skill, you bring your *machine*."

"I'll see you then. Goodnight."

John didn't answer.

"You do have veto power if you don't like what you see. Bryan didn't mention it for a reason," Michael said.

"Good to know, and thanks for your confidence in me."

Michael and Alex said goodnight to Elan and John. Elan was wound tight.

"Let it go, Elan, I know how strongly you feel about it, but majority rules in this group. It's what we wanted, to do it right this time, not like the mess on Earth."

"I'm sorry, John. What I hoped for was you got sick, and then I could fly the ship like we did in the simulator."

John laughed.

"*Everybody* wants my job, unless something goes wrong."

They walked into the elevator and John pressed SHIP.

"You want some company?" Elan asked.

"No, get some sleep."

The elevator doors opened, and Elan left for his quarters.

"Goodnight, John."

John walked to the flight deck. Hunter leaned on his elbow in the command chair. Rhian tried to repair a loose switch. Susan looked through a flight manual on her tablet. George sat with his arms folded.

"Hey, John, we listened to the meeting with Trent. If it means anything, I'm with you," Hunter said.

"What if something were to happen to the Robonaut, like a broken wire," George asked.

"That reminds me, has anyone seen my wire cutters?" Ricky asked.

"Wow, I spent a few years with you guys, and I never knew you were evil."

"John?"

"Yes, Trent?"

"Let's separate the ship right now while they're asleep."

"I'd be the first colonist hung on Titan."

Cary Allen Stone

Chapter 7

The GLs relocated the colonists to the GR. By the afternoon, the flight deck was called, and told all the colonists were out of the FRMs.

"Okay, they're in position back there. Let's get to work. Is EPM up?"

"We're ready, Commander."

As they had trained for so many times in the simulator, the crew worked with the engineers to separate the FRMs from the ship. Each FRM was the length from behind the GR at mid-ship to the EFTs. The FRMs would descend in a sequential order. The outer most FRMs would go first. FRM–1's electromagnetic locks were disengaged and the blow bolts detonated. The FRMs, like the Shuttle, hovered, and then moved to the side guided by its auto-land system. It used air-pressure thrusters to maneuver. Once clear, the FRM began a controlled descent. Four landing struts extended before touchdown. The remaining FRMs were next. The entire procedure was flawless thanks to Hinkle. It took three hours to complete the mission.

The crew celebrated.

John had flown a variety of aircraft from civilian commercial planes to high-tech, top-secret military aircraft. He flew through all kinds of weather, to every continent on Earth, seen and done things in the sky, which would frighten average folks. John was the first commander of a SEEDS ship, but the separation of the ship from the GR was given to the Robonaut. The call was made for Robert to bring the Robonaut to the flight deck.

"I've written papers on everything from black holes to the Theory of Everything, and what will I be remembered for? I witnessed a *Transhuman* separate the ship from the GR," Trent said.

"At least you'll be remembered. I was dropped from the history books, replaced by Robonaut. Did Ricky ever find his wire cutters?" John asked.

Michael entered the flight deck.

"John are you ready for the separation? Where's Robert and the robot?"

"Robert forget to build a clock into his *Not-Human*?"

"You can always veto."

"It better listen to every command."

Alex entered the flight deck.

"Hello, John, Trent, crew."

"Michael?"

"Yes, Trent?"

"You've overseen SEEDS for a long time. What do you plan to do on Titan?"

"One step at a time, we're not on Titan yet. We have a lot to do before the colony is habitable. I haven't reflected on it, why?"

"Well, once the colony is operational, you will have the solar system at your fingertips. You will be free to do all the research you ever wanted on Titan. I love it on the ship, and I'll love to be on Titan. I look out my dome, and see the universe from a perspective I've always wanted to see it, not in a book, or on a computer, it's right out my window. I'm a graphene's width away and can almost touch it."

Michael stood next to Alex. On Titan, Michael Talbot, the astrophysicist, and Alex Arthur, the physicist, could pursue knowledge like they planned to in their careers, instead of babysitting PhD's. They had spoken to Britte, and he promised to put them first on the list for a space condominium with spacious living areas away from the colony.

"In 2013, the scientists at the Institute of Astrophysics detected polycyclic aromatic hydrocarbons in Titan's atmosphere, which suggested a possible precursor for life, something to research," Trent said.

"Excellent suggestion," Alex said.

The Transhuman and its master arrived. Robert walked into the flight deck alone. John had a flash of hope, but Robonaut stood outside the door.

"Good morning, Alex, Michael, John."

"Bring *It* in and let's get this over with. As soon as the ship is free of the GR, the ship is mine."

"Okay, John, no problem. I only need a brief time to show Michael what my Transhuman can do. It doesn't want your job. You do need to know a few things about him though. My engrams are linked to his machinery and every instruction passes through logic trees. If you're not sure he deciphered a command, explain it to me, and I will translate for him. It's how it learns."

"This is one hell of a time for *It* to *learn*."

"Please be clear on what you want him to do."

"Get *It* into the captain's chair."

The Transhuman sat, its cyborg's hand rested on the control grip. It appeared look at the PFD. John sat in the command chair and leaned forward to give the Robonaut directions. He spoke to it clear and slow, explained what the cyborg was to do and in what order. He told it what to watch for on the instrument panel.

"Pay attention to the PFD and follow its guidance."

John turned toward Robert.

"Do you think *It* understood what I said?"

"Sounded straightforward to me, so it sounded straightforward to him."

"Is everyone ready?"

Each of his crew replied "Affirmative."

"We'll only engage one engine. Read the Engine Start Checklist."

The crew completed the items.

"Engine ON."

Rhian reached across the panel.

"Disengage the locks, and blow the bolts on all four GR struts. Idle power on the thrusters."

The struts were a foot away from the main ship.

"Robonaut, the ship is free of the GR struts. Proceed with your instructions."

The Transhuman monitored the PFD.

It had to keep the guide bars centered. If the horizontal guide bar rose, the Robonaut pushed forward on the control grip to bring the guide bar back down to the center. If the lateral guide bar moved right, the Robonaut would move the control grip left until the guide bar centered. If the guide bars deviated more than a quarter degree, the struts would impact the ship.

Rhian read the distance remaining to the aft end of the ship, so they knew when the ship was clear of the GR.

"804 m's, 228 m's, 153 m's, 76 m's, 30 m's, 9 m's, 3 m's...

Trent monitored through his dome and kept an eye on his LMI to verify the distance matched with Rhian's callouts.

"Robonaut, disengage the control grip. Get *it* out of my seat."

John sat in the captain seat. The ship continued to move forward from minimum thrust.

"Shut down SE-1."

"Shutdown, Commander."

"Verify maneuvering SE-15 is forward."

"Maneuvering SE-15 forward, Commander."

"Engage the maneuvering SE-15."

The ship began to stop.

"Shut down maneuvering SE-15."

"Shutdown, Commander."

"Engage Auto-Flight."

"Engaged, Commander."

The ship was free of the GR.

Hunter sat in the command chair, but John was still in command. He turned to Robert. The Robonaut was outside the door.

"Now tell your machine to get out *It's* wrenches. *It* has subservient labor to do."

John objected to calling it anything "human."

"You are welcome, John, from the both of us."

Robert turned to leave but stopped where Michael stood.

"What do you think of my Robonaut now?"

"I look forward to it working with its partner connecting the FRMs."

Robert, not amused, marched his creation to the cargo module.

Michael closed the flight deck door. He and Alex enjoyed the crew's conversation in progress.

"We never needed *It*," Hunter said.

"Well, *It's* done," Ricky said.

"We can talk about *It* later. Trent, what do you think?" John asked.

"Someone should *unscrew It*!"

"Thank you, Trent, and crew, for assisting with the separation, and for believing in me."

"We're with you 100%, Commander," Rhian said.

John knew he could have done the maneuver.

"John, I relayed the completion of the separation to Bryan and Isaac. First chance I get, I will tell them what I thought of their decision," Trent said.

"Let it go, no one will remember centuries from now."

"They won't have to wait centuries, John, didn't you see the camera Bob installed?" Michael asked.

"Camera?"

John turned and Michael pointed at the camera, which broadcasted live to the colonists.

"Brenda told the colonists she would get Bob to install a camera on the flight deck, so they could watch on the monitors he put throughout the ship."

Brenda walked in. Ricky laughed.

"Turn it off. I want to speak to Brenda without witnesses."

"What's wrong?" she asked.

John pointed at the camera.

"Oh, Bob *did* put one in."

"Thanks, John," Michael said.

"For what?"

John made Michael's life easier because he did not veto the Transhuman decision.

"You are a friend first, and always."

Michael smiled. Alex stood next to him.

"You too, Alex. Is Elan still in the Shuttle?"

"I'm in contact with him," Trent said.

"Are we ready to disengage the Shuttle?"

"Yes, Sir, all systems are green," George said.

"Elan, Shuttle is disengaged," Trent said.

"Roger that, SEEDS–2025."

Rhian pressed the switch.

The shuttle hovered then began its descent to the surface. It maneuvered next to the FRMs. The rest of Base Crater was available to land the ship.

Once John received confirmation Elan was on the surface, he began the descent.

Thirty-four bulky landing struts extended from below SEEDS–2025, two set of gear for each module of the main ship

John took all the time in the new world to let the

ship descend at a rate, which would not cause a cataclysmic ending. The maneuver demanded courage, and precision.

Elan observed the ship's descent.

"You should be below the clouds now. I see the you."

Rhian counted down with the GPR. Trent verified on the LMI.

The ship contacted the surface of Titan.

After seven years of SEEDS, World War Last, and hundreds of millions of miles, they were home.

The crew and Titanauts celebrated.

The colonists were anxious to see their new home, and the surrounding landscape.

Saturn dominated half of the moon's sky. For humans who had looked at a sun the size of a basketball their entire lives, they were awed by the view.

The next step in the colonization of Titan began.

After a long ride secured in their racks, except for the one time Robonaut sang "Happy *Irthday*" to John, both Robonauts made their way to the large cargo airlock, and waited for the pressurization to drop, so the sizable cargo door could open.

After the door dropped to the surface, the Robonauts exited down the extended ramp and secured the FRMs together.

When completed, the modules were powered, and pressurized.

The Robonauts used the graphene panels to construct the geodesic dome.

With the dome built, the Robonauts created an

airlock from the structure to the ship.

The engineers asked Dr. Hammerstein where to place the defensive weapons for the maximum protection of the colony.

Bob, and his team, found the best place to set up the Titan Communications Center.

Phillip's team put the final touches on the new colony by using the 10-D printers to construct new laboratories, and install common area amenities.

The Robonauts returned to transport the large fish farm tank, the animal shelter, the hydroponics station, and the Medical Station to their proper places inside the facility.

A waste water system outside of the dome was piped through the hydroponic wells, and fish farm then through a filtration, and purification system before being pumped into a reservoir.

While the Robonauts built the dome, Phillip's 10-D printer built a freshwater tank for the water in the sleeves between the hulls.

Once the massive tank was in position, the engineers pumped freshwater to fill it.

One of the first explorations the colonists would make would be to find water on Titan, whether they melted, and treated the ice, or dug hundreds of kilometers down to reach a subterranean ocean.

Their second exploration of the moon would be to try and locate the Huygen's impact site.

As the human worker's returned to the ship, they remained in quarantine until they passed Dr. Baker's DOI.

A final conference was held with the engineers. They had certified the structure habitable by humans, and the live animals.

Bryan and Isaac put on their NewGen NASA spacesuits.

They exited down the ramp and stood outside the dome. With both their hands holding it, they planted the SEEDS flag, and declared ownership of Titan.

Representative Britte, and Vice Representative Winslow led the Titanauts in a procession to their new home. John and his crew followed them. The colonists could hardly contain their excitement as they walked into the pressurized structure.

They removed their helmets, and began to roam to locate their eggs. They looked with wonderment at a facility as large as a stadium on Earth, with every life support function met.

The colonists thanked John and his crew for getting them safely to Titan, and to tell John how funny it was to watch his reaction when he learned the camera was behind him on the flight deck.

Those who entered the colony and were spiritual, said a prayer. Those who weren't, also said a prayer.

Michael and Alex stood to the side, away from the crowd.

"Alex, this is home."

"No, Michael, this is *our* home!"

Their fingers intertwined.

Months passed.

Michael and Alex sat with John.

"I get the feeling you like Titan," John said.

"I feel like I was always supposed to be here," Michael said.

Alex rested her head on his shoulder.

"It's peaceful here."

"Dad's gone, but he would have liked it here. I miss knocking down a few beers with him sitting on the back porch. To think none of it exists any longer on Earth, it's such a shame, but I know he's in the universe, a better place."

"What do you plan to do on Titan, John?" Alex asked.

"Oh, that's easy, I've been thinking about it since we left Earth."

"Well, what is it?"

"I'm going to open the first pub, and brew beer. 'The Finest Ale in the Universe.' I'm going to build a back porch like we had at dad's house, and invite people to sit, drink my brew, and watch Saturn turn."

"Alex and I want to ask you for a favor, something special."

"Anything, Michael, name it."

Michael looked at Alex.

"John Kelly, as commander of the historical ship SEEDS–2025, we request you perform the ceremony of marriage for us," Alex said.

"I've never performed the ceremony, but I can get what I need off the computer.

Brenda walked up and took John's hand.

The ceremony would go into the history books as the first on Titan. Word spread fast.

Everyone gathered in the dome. John wore his formal uniform, his crew the same.

With Saturn filling the graphene windows, Michael met Alex in front of John. Brenda was Alex's bridesmaid, and Elan was Michael's best man.

Lukas played Holst's, *The Planets: Saturn, the Bringer of Old Age*.

Elan handed Michael one of the Rings of Saturn. Michael slid it on Alex's finger. Brenda handed Alex the other, and she slid it on Michael's finger.

Commander John Kelly said the words to bind the union, and both celebrants confirmed their commitment to each other with an "A–O.K."

Isaac stood next to Bryan, tearful. He never believed he would see Titan, much less live to see Alex, and Michael's ceremony.

The Robonauts completed the drilling operation inside the dome.

The seven-level deep cavern resembled the SEEDS' facility, only inverted.

All science labs occupied the lowest levels. Engineering, and the 10-D printers occupied the top levels for easy access. Each level's secondary purpose was to provide shelter in the event of a catastrophic event, or an attack.

Engineering and Fabrication used the cave-dwelling concept to create residences in the walls of Base Crater close to the dome.

The dome became the community play space. KELLY'S PUB was the favorite venue.

Their arrival on Titan ended the "No relationship/children rule." The dome was filled with families. Children darted between adult legs.

At a planning hearing, Phillip presented a plan for the Gravity Ring.

"We should tether the GR now, and bring it down as far as possible *into* the cloud layer. We don't know what became of the Russians and Chinese. Let's not give them an easy way to find us."

The vote was unanimous.

Phillip asked Elan to work with Engineering to construct a hyperloop system between facilities, Base Crater's cave-dweller-styled homes, and to "suburban" homes Alex and Michael lived in. He also placed track for exploration.

After the first Titan year, they discussed splitting the kilometer-long SEEDS–2025 in two.

Some colonists considered returning to Earth after the radiation abated.

The explorers planned a journey to as far as Proxima B.

They also considered traveling to another Saturn moon. "Mimas" was a *prolate*, meaning its shape resembled the damaged "Death Star" from the film. It suffered a direct hit from an asteroid, which left a crater the size Australia. It was believed to have an abundant supply of *water ice*, something of great interest to the colonists. The weather there was more agreeable.

Bob's weather station tracked a methane rainstorm. The colony was in its path. Anyone working outside, including the Robonauts, found shelter in the dome, or residences. The methane rain was corrosive. After the storm passed, the engineers checked the metamaterials and flexible gel, which coated the exteriors of the facilities.

Bob positioned a satellite in geosynchronous orbit above the Gravity Ring. Like the SETI antenna on Earth, it pinged the galaxy searching for signals.

On the day before the first anniversary of the colony, it received one, in what sounded like Russian.

The ComCen researcher monitoring the satellite, ran to get Bob who ran back with him to hear the transmission.

When Bob heard the faint call, his eyes went wide. He called Michael.

The Talbot's arrived via the Mini-Loop, and joined with him in ComCen to listen.

The signal was weak, almost undetectable. Bob boosted the audio.

"Sounds Russian, but I'm not sure," he said.

He ran it through a translator. Michael saw fear in Bob's eyes.

"КРАСНАЯ ЗВЕЗДА 1, MAYDAY!"

"It's a Mayday from the Russian ship."

Michael told Bryan about the transmission.

Within an hour, Bryan, Isaac, Elan, Phillip, and John met with Alex, Michael, and Bob in the ComCen located inside the dome.

"You're positive it translated to a Mayday from the Russians?" Bryan asked.

Phillip was shaken. He never expected, as the Representative, to be dealing with an adversary, nor did the others.

They considered it a possibility, but a remote one.

Trent walked in and listened to the transmission.

"Трахать!" Trent said.

He surprised them.

"You speak Russian?" Isaac asked.

"And six other languages, but that's not important now. How long have they been transmitting?"

"Jimmy heard the first one about an hour ago. It's been repeating since," Bob said.

"Could the signal be from Mars?" Michael asked.

"When I first heard it, I conjectured it might be, a transmitter still powered, left after a failed colony on Mars. Further analysis revealed the signal's distance is changing. It's coming closer," Bob said.

"Do not reply," John said.

"There might be casualties, people dying. We can't ignore it. What if it were us making the call?" Alex asked.

"Sorry, Alex, I'm with John on this," Elan said.

"I agree. We don't have enough information yet," Bryan said.

"Good thing we followed William's advice, and lowered the GR into the cloud cover," Steven said.

Bryan looked at Isaac. They communicated without saying a word.

"I don't want to put our people into jeopardy. If the Russians and Chinese destroyed each other on Mars, and some survived, why would we want them here?" Phillip asked.

"We don't know what kind of super-predators they've become. We can't be the only colony with a Transhuman, and maybe theirs doesn't sing 'Happy Irthday.' If the Chinese and Russians fought it out on Mars, what makes us believe they wouldn't kill us? I think you said it, Isaac, back in SEEDS, 'We're scientists, not soldiers,'" Elan said.

"We could send a representative who can evaluate the situation, return, and if need be then take them out with the RGs," Bryan said.

"Who's going to volunteer for that suicide mission?" Phillip asked.

"I will," Alex said.

"Alex, if they're hostile, they could take you hostage. How do we negotiate our way out of that?" Michael asked.

"I agree, Alex, it's too big a gamble," Isaac said.

"What about sending the Robonaut?" Phillip asked.

"Let the Robonaut take the risk. Hammerstein could rig him to blow if it got ugly," Elan said.

He stirred mental deliberations.

"No, because they could download all of Robert's microchip, including all the information about the colony, our weaknesses, and our defenses. Don't forget, I blew away the ISS with their people on board. I doubt they are reaching out to make friends. We'd be committing colonial suicide," John said.

"John's right. We can't take that chance. After all we've done to get here, and build a life here to continue our exploration of the universe? It would be foolish to assume, they have good intentions, especially if they fought on Mars," Bryan said.

"Good point," Isaac said.

"What if we allow one of them to come here, find out what they want?" Alex asked.

"You still expose our location, and give them valuable intel," John said.

"What if there are women and children on their ship?" Alex asked.

"What about *our* women and children, and protecting them? That's *my* job," John said.

"We could go silent, turn off all electronic signatures. Let them fly past," Bob said.

"We could shelter in place in the Levels until they're gone," Phillip said.

"Bob, they knew we were headed here before we left," John said.

"Send Robonaut to intimidate them. If they mean us harm, the Robonaut can end it there. If they don't, as Alex believes, then we welcome them," Elan said.

"You'd leave the decision up to the Robonaut?" Michael asked.

"No, Robert can look through its eyes, evaluate the situation *then* proceed from there," Alex said.

"If they made it to Mars, we must also assume they aren't afraid of the Robonaut, or have their own Transhuman, maybe more than two," John said.

Alex was frustrated. The men were ready to fire on the ship without speaking to the Russians.

"We left Earth *with* humanity in our hearts, to build a better world than the one we left behind. And in a heartbeat, we turn primal? Lose our humanity? What was the point of coming here? To be like they were on Earth?" Alex asked.

"We also brought our intellects. Do we allow an aggressor to take our colony, end our mission to explore the universe from Titan?" Elan asked.

"Even if they seek refuge, what about viruses, and diseases?" Steven asked.

"Anyway you look at it, it comes down to survival. They decided their fate long ago, as did we. Darwinian principals apply here," Bryan said.

"Can't we find out what they want? They may have scientists, and engineers we need, technology we don't have," Alex said.

The discussion froze, both arguments were strong.

"We have time to think this through. Let's run the scenarios through the computers to determine which course of action is best," Bryan said.

"When do I inform the colonists?" Phillip asked.

"After we have a course of action," John said.

They broke up into groups.

Bryan and Isaac spoke together.

Elan agonized with John.

Phillip and Steven tried to think of another option.

Bob walked away alone.

Alex and Michael discussed it outside of the ComCen.

"I don't want to leave them to die. If you were on their ship, you might have a different opinion, Michael. They could be desperate. What if there are children on the ship?"

"If we can find a way to determine they're not a threat, we take them in."

"My head hurts," Alex said.

"Thinking does that."

Bryan and Isaac went to their office. Isaac asked Trent to join them. They entered the data into the computers.

"Interesting equation. Shakespeare said it long ago, 'To be, or not to be,'" Trent said.

"To be, I hope," Bryan said.

"You quote the Bard? A non-scientist?" Isaac asked.

"I predict you won't get the answer out of the computers. Your programming the computers with speculations, not empirical evidence. It's more probable, after a failed colony on Mars, the Russians are desperate, and capable of the worst," Trent said.

"Let's assume they have a hundred survivors. Can we shelter them? Can we feed them? Can we live in peace?" Bryan asked.

Isaac entered parameters into the computer.

"A hundred colonists would put an immediate strain on our resources. As far as shelter, they could land next to SEEDS-2025, and live in their ship until Dr. Baker does a DOI. If there are none, they could live in the Levels until Willian constructs habitats," Trent said.

"What's to stop them from landing on the other side of Titan, and planning an attack on our colony?" Isaac asked.

"All interesting equations," Bryan said.

Phillip and Steven walked into the dome from ComCen.

"This is one time I *don't* want to be the Representative."

"The Russians and Chinese know we went to Titan, but they don't know if we survived. They're also taking a chance we don't destroy them first," Steven said.

"Bob's satellite would appear to them we did survive."

"We could direct the RGs at their ship as they get closer, and take them out like we did with the ISS. John reacted with no envoy. Call it operational necessity," Steven said.

Elan and John went to the pub, and sat in a booth. They kept their voices down, so as not to cause a *pre*-panic.

"Send the Robonaut. You owe Robert one."

"There is one other option."

"Send Hinkle?" Elan asked.

"No, the other option is...I go."

"Are you insane? Too much home brew? Why would you take the chance?"

"Because, I'm the Commander. I'm responsible for the safety of the colony. I'm also trained to fight, so are my WCSs."

"It could be a suicide mission. Let the Robonaut get whacked. Robert can build another one, but no one can build another John Kelly."

Brenda saw them, walked over, and sat next to John.

"What's with the serious faces?"

"Tell her, John, Brenda's crew."

"Tomorrow."

"No, now, she needs to know. In ten hours, everyone in the colony will know, what's the difference?"

"Tell me what?"

John leaned close to her and lowered his voice.

"Bob's SETI satellite pinged the Russians today. They declared a Mayday."

"Uh-oh."

"Yeah."

"Now what?"

"We'll know in about an hour, or two. Bryan and Isaac entered possible scenarios into the computers," Elan said.

"One suggestion was to hide, another to engage, and a third was to send the Robonaut to investigate," John said.

"But John proposed another option just now. He wants to go and find out what they want."

"Not *my* John."

"Yes, *your* John. I'm the logical choice. I don't think the Robonaut will be able to deal with them, Transhuman to human. It *has* to be me."

"No, it doesn't *have* to be you. I didn't come all this way to fall in love with you, only to have you killed by the Russians!"

"I'm the one who ordered the attack on the ISS. I should be the one to face them. Besides, I'm still in command. I make the calls."

"You better think long and hard about it, John."

"We may not have time to think too long," John said.

"I agree with Brenda, John."

Bob sat alone in his office and waited for the results. He felt responsible because he launched the satellite. He would have spoken up, but he didn't think anyone wanted to hear what he had to say.

An hour passed. They regathered in ComCen. John spoke before anyone else did.

"I'm going to their ship, discussion over. I surrendered my command to the Robonaut once. It was a mistake. I'm not doing it again, and if they must be destroyed, it will be my call as the Commander of SEEDS-2025."

The others studied him.

"I'm against John going, and I'm against a strike on their ship until we know who is on it, and what their intentions are," Alex said.

John didn't back of, nor did Elan.

"Alex, we can't take the chance they're *harmless*. Let them continue into deep space," Elan said.

"Nothing's stopping them from landing without asking for our permission, then what?" Michael asked.

"What did the computers say to do?" Phillip asked.

"50/50," Bryan said.

"Why do we keep relying on the computers and Transhumans? *Humans* should decide this. Bob, can you shut down the satellite?" John asked.

"Sure."

"Do it. If they plan to touchdown on Titan, without asking, we won't make it easy for them."

Bob went into the computer room. He returned five minutes later.

"It's down."

Alex shook her head.

"This needs to be explained to the colonists now. I suggest Alex tell them. The decision is not only up to us, that's what we agreed to," Isaac said.

"Why me?"

"Because, my daughter, our testosterone may be overpowering our intellects. We don't know *all* the answers."

"I'll send out an emergency notice to meet in the dome in one hour," Phillip said.

He and Steven left. John looked at Alex.

"If they vote in favor of engaging the Russians—"

"I know, we kill them all," Alex said.

"I say John should decide our response. We've trusted John's decisions to get us to Titan. We should trust him to make the right decision now," Bryan said.

Bryan, Isaac, Elan, and John had a quiet conversation. Bob went to the control room.

Alex and Michael went to the pub, and were greeted by Brenda.

"What's it going to be?" she asked.

"We'll know in an hour," Michael said.

"You'll know what you want to drink in an hour?"

They realized their nerves were stretched tight.

"Two of John's brews, please."

"It's all we have, good choice."

Brenda went to the bar.

"Remember what the ISS did? They launched without provocation, with no meeting to discuss how to share the galaxy."

"Does that give us the right to be the bad guys? Aren't we better than that?"

"Sometimes bad actions are required to protect good people. What if when the missile came at us, and John turned the other cheek? We wouldn't be here right now."

"I get it. I do. I don't see why we can't *talk* to them first."

"What if they arrive above Base Crater, make some request for our help, and then blow us into the universe?"

Brenda placed two mugs in front of them.

"So, why do you two have looks like it's the end of the world?" Brenda asked.

"I'll tell you after I finish my beer," Alex said.

Brenda knew the meeting didn't go well. Bryan and Isaac walked in.

"Two more, please," Bryan said.

"Think we'll feel any better after the beer?" Isaac asked.

"No," Bryan said.

The signal got stronger, the Mayday repeated. Bob turned the volume off. He knew the Russians were coming straight to them.

Hope John takes them out with the RGs.

Cary Allen Stone

Chapter 8

The colonists strolled into the dome.

Kids played, and parents watched over them.

The older colonists enjoyed the community atmosphere, and the peace they had on Titan.

Before the meeting was to start, all but three had arrived.

Phillip stood on the riser with Alex. They exchanged pleasantries with friends.

As he called the meeting to order, the three missing colonists burst through the doors.

"Thank you for coming. I know you had other things to do, but this will be the most important meeting we ever have. What you will hear is very serious. After we provide you with the details, you will be required to vote, so please give us your undivided attention."

He watched their facial expressions change.

"Alex will tell you about it. Please reserve your questions until she is finished. Alex."

She walked forward and looked at the children who fidgeted in their seats, or on laps.

She saw concerned looks on the adults.

"Thank you, Phillip. Earlier today, Michael and I received a call from Bob in the ComCen. We rushed there. For those who may not know, Bob, after we landed on Titan, launched a satellite into orbit that surveys the galaxy for signals, much like SETI once did on Earth."

Bryan, Isaac, Elan, Michael, Bob, and John stood off to the side, and studied reactions.

"Bob heard a faint signal. After he boosted reception, and ran it through the translator, he realized it was a Mayday call."

A communal gasp was heard.

"The signal came from the Russian ship that traveled to Mars."

Heads turned.

"It's still faint, but Bob says it's getting closer. Phillip, Steven, Bryan, my dad, Elan, John, Michael and I discussed its *implications*."

The dome was void of any sounds other than Alex's words.

"Our discussion revolved around whether to answer their distress call. Right now, we're divided. Some say we shouldn't answer considering our last encounter with the Russians. They attacked us as we left for Titan, and we destroyed their ISS. There is reason to believe they are hostile, possibly planning to take our colony after failing in theirs. And there are those who want to reach out and do what we can to help them."

Murmurs spread.

"It was suggested sending the Robonaut to determine their intentions. Commander Kelly decided he should go, and have a *human* encounter with them. It they are hostile, we will destroy them with the RGs and lasers, like the ISS."

Discussions grew louder among the colonists.

"*Please*, now is not the time to argue with each other! Now is the time to think."

"Take them out!" a man said.

His kids gathered around his legs, his wife was at his side.

Let's find out what they want?" an older man said.

"We should help them," a woman said.

More terse callouts were shouted.

The room felt like a glacier of fear.

People roiled.

Dr. Baker expected an increase in anxiety Nanos.

Alex asked for quiet.

John walked onto the riser.

"I will attempt to make contact while they are still a great distance from us. If I decide they are hostile, I will order a first strike. If it's decided they are not a threat to us, I will go to speak with them."

Bryan went to the riser next.

"You have believed in Isaac, and me to get you here. We've come too far to lose everything now. I support John's decisions."

Isaac stepped onto the riser.

"I agree with John."

Elan stepped onto the riser.

"So do I."

Steven joined them.

"John should make the decision."

Michael joined Alex.

"Alex and I believe we should at least speak with them, before any action is taken. If we don't find out what they want, killing them will only haunt us until the day we die," Michael said.

Phillip took over the meeting.

"John has a point, but we all decided to live in a democracy where every colonist has a vote. Go home. Discuss among yourselves and your loved ones. Consider all the options Alex presented. Don't let your emotions think for you. In two hours, I want you to vote. We will tally the votes, and proceed accordingly."

The colonists filed out in silence.

John pulled Hammerstein aside.

"I need to be certain the Rail Guns will destroy the Russian ship from here."

"You'll only need one to rupture the hull, the vacuum of space will do the rest."

"I'll need your oversight over the two crew members who will discharge the RGs and lasers, unless you don't want to place yourself in danger."

"I will assist, Commander."

"How do you feel about this?"

"I concur with you, Commander."

"One more question. What kind of weapons can I expect on the Russian ship?"

"Expect an advanced targeting system since they left Earth."

"I also need you to make a suicide vest for me with enough explosives to blow a hole in their ship."

"I'll have it by morning, Commander."

Two hours later, they waited for the results of the vote in Phillip's office.

He sat at his community computer.

After every colonist submitted a vote, Phillip looked
up from the computer screen.

"Our initial prediction was off by 10%, Bryan. After the computer evaluated the data entered, it decided the odds were 52% in favor of action versus 48% in favor of talking with them," Isaac said.

"Now, we do it my way," John said.

Elan looked at each of them.

"I don't see any other choice."

"Unless we send the Robonaut," Michael said.

"I came up with another reason not to use the Robonaut. Let's say they are seeking assistance and are harmless. We don't know what their reaction would be to the Robonaut. If I asked for help and saw Robonaut, I would assume those who sent him were hostile. No, I'll go, human to human, a consolation for Alex," John said.

"What are you thinking, Alex?"" Bryan asked.

"It doesn't matter. The colonists voted, and John is in command. Maybe, you all are right. I don't know anymore."

"What if we call, and they don't answer, and they launch?" Bob asked.

"They left Mars to find a home. They gain nothing by destroying our colony," Phillip said.

Robert and Trent walked into the office.

"What was the outcome of the vote?" Trent asked.

"278-42 in favor of a first strike," Phillip said.

"We're not using the Robonaut, Robert," Elan said.

"I agree. It would be a mistake to use Robonaut. He'll be needed to rebuild the colony if we're attacked, assuming we survive."

The others were surprised at his answer.

They had expected an argument.

"Living off-Earth has led to the speciation of the people. I'm interested to find out if our children are being re-engineered," Trent said.

Bob walked in from the ComCen.

"Bob, can our transmitter reach the Russian ship?" John asked.

"They're still far away. You might want to wait until tomorrow when they're closer."

"What a shame to be in this situation. It created a division among the colonists. I don't think anyone expected to face off with the Russians. I watched an entire mood change on the faces in the dome," Trent said.

"It's no different than it was on Earth, good versus evil. The conflict has been around since the universe was born," John said.

Alex agreed.

"When do you want to make contact?" Bryan asked.

"Bob's right, tomorrow morning, after a good night's sleep, if possible. We will prepare for the worst, and hope for the best."

"Something bad happened on the Red Planet. Maybe it wasn't as conducive to colonization as everyone thought. Maybe the Chinese and Russians couldn't get along," Alex said.

"What do you think happened to the Chinese?"

Trent asked.

"Since it's the Russians in the ship, one would assume the Chinese forced them out. It may have gone nuclear like on Earth," Isaac said.

"I have to make an announcement to the colonists about the outcome of the vote," Phillip said.

"What do you want me to do, John?" Bob asked.

"Be in ComCen early and find out how close they are. I'll make the call to the ship at 9:00."

"I'll be there, John."

"Phillip, Steven, I want all the colonists to take shelter in the Levels. Make sure there is enough food and water to last for a while. Have Dr. Baker set up a triage there. My crew will man the Rail Guns, and the lasers. I already spoke with Dr. Hammerstein. He's agreed to work with my crew."

John looked at Alex and Michael.

"Would you two help Phillip with the announcement?"

"Sure, John," Michael said.

They left to make the announcement from Phillip's office.

"Elan, will you make sure the Shuttle is prepared for launch?"

"Affirmative."

"What do you want me to do," Trent asked.

"Think. You're great at it. See if you can find other options, another course of action."

"Does anyone else beside me speak Russian?" Trent asked.

No one did.

"I also speak Mandarin in the event the Chinese show up next."

"I'll need you in the ComCen to translate if needed."

"I'll be there, John."

"Okay, from here on, my crew and I will be on high alert status. The rest of you should stop by the pub before going home to sleep. It could be the last time you get to taste my brew."

"Good idea, John, come on, Bryan, let's go talk about the good old days, while we can still remember them," Isaac said.

John, Elan, and Trent remained.

"I don't think you should go alone, John," Elan said.

"Seconded. We should form a boarding party. You, me as the interpreter, Dr. Baker if they need medical attention, and so he can do a DOI. Elan in case they have mechanical problems," Trent said.

"Not on the first Shuttle. We'll know from the call if I need an interpreter. If they are not a threat, you, Elan, and Baker will be on the next Shuttle."

John didn't mention what he would take with him to the ship.

"I still think we should do a preemptive strike," Elan said.

"That question will be answered when I call."

They left and headed for the pub.

As they walked in, they saw Bryan and Isaac at the bar. Both looked like they had aged fifty years since they arrived on Titan. Trent knew they had spoken days earlier to Fulbright about pasting their engrams on microchips.

Wonder if Isaac told Alex.

Brenda was in the pub. She saw John walk in.

"You're going to talk to the Russians, possibly go up to their ship. I think it's a bad idea."

"If anything happens, I need you here to take command, which reminds me, would you get the crew in here? I need to discuss tomorrow with them."

She walked away distressed, and contacted them. John walked behind the bar and poured two for Elan, and Trent.

"John, it's been a wild ride since I met you," Elan said.

"Can you construct a Maxi-Loop to Mimas for us to escape on tomorrow?"

"You always did like my *AirTran*."

"Did you ever give Bryan a ride on it?"

"Oh, I forgot to give him a ride."

Humor and cold beer always helped stressful conditions. An hour later, the entire SEEDS crew walked into the pub.

"Hey, John, what's the word?" Ricky asked.

"Titan, we have a problem."

"Actually, what Swigert said on Apollo 13 was, 'Okay, Houston, we've had a problem here,'" Ricky said.

John wasn't in the mood.

Morning came on Titan.

All the primary characters arrived in the ComCen.

Bob sat at a computer array, and listened on headphones until he picked up the Mayday.

"Want headphones?" Bob asked.

"No, thanks."

He switched to the speakers.

It was silent in the room, except for the background crackling noise from the distant ship.

John held the mic, and Trent stood next to him.

"What if it's a ghost ship by now," Trent asked.

"If it were a ghost ship, how did it find us, and not crash on a planet, moon, or fly by?" Elan asked.

"The only way to answer the question is to answer the call," John said.

He looked at Phillip.

"Are all the colonists accounted for, and in the Levels?"

"Checked twice, John."

He used planetary communications to check on his crew."

"Everyone in place?"

"TwoBears at Rail Gun 1."

"Tinsdale at Rail Gun 2."

"Chan at lasers."

Hammerstein met with John and handed him the vest. He left to monitor George and Ricky by the RGs. Danny was about ten meters away.

Hunter, Lukas, and Sean stood by the fission reactor and verified the connection was secure to the RGs.

Edward, and Hank floated between them in case they were needed.

Brenda, Rhian, and Susan monitored the colonists in the Levels.

Parents kept their children quiet and close.

Nervous adults paced.

Dr. Baker, and his medical personnel handed out bedside manner.

Amygdala's cascaded changes to their bodies. The hormones, cortisol, and adrenaline, surged and boosted their motor muscles. Tachypsychia slowed the speed of their minds. They thought about the Russian ship.

"КРАСНАЯ ЗВЕЗДА 1, КРАСНАЯ ЗВЕЗДА 1" Trent said.

John followed.

"RED STAR 1, do you copy, RED STAR 1?"

"КРАСНАЯ ЗВЕЗДА 1, КРАСНАЯ ЗВЕЗДА 1?" Trent said.

"RED STAR 1, do you copy, RED STAR 1?"

The frequency had background noise, but they did not receive a reply.

"Bob can you boost the signal?"

Bob turned it to the maximum setting. John transmitted again. Silence, except for the background sizzle. The MAYDAY ceased to be repeated.

"Maybe it *is* a ghost ship," John said.

"If it is, our worries have been mitigated," Trent said.

They waited for thirty minutes. They had proffered several scenarios, but the Russian ship *not* responding wasn't one of them. They tried again.

"КРАСНАЯ ЗВЕЗДА 1, КРАСНАЯ ЗВЕЗДА 1?"

"RED STAR 1, do you copy, RED STAR 1?"

Silence. After several more attempts to reach the ship, John turned to Bob.

"Record our next transmission, make a loop, and broadcast it for the next eight hours."

"I already recorded it."

"Thanks, Bob. Trent, in eight hours we will assume it *is* a ghost ship."

"This entire Russian ship thing is an enigma. It's looking more like a ghost ship, but the odds of this turning out right are astronomical."

"Astronomical odds are better than none. It's definitely a *trip wire* situation," John said.

Trent gave an obligatory smile.

Those in ComCen waited.

"If we do not get a response in the next eight hours, Elan, Trent, Clifford, George, and I will take the Shuttle to the Russian ship to determine its status."

"Phillip, please tell Clifford he's going along."

"I want to go, John," Alex said.

"Negative."

"Why can't I go? Michael?"

John turned to Michael.

"Both of us want to go, John."

"I need Elan for engineering, Trent to translate, Clifford to do a DOI, and if a doctor is needed, and George for muscle. The Shuttle carries six, even if I agreed to take you only one of you could go."

"Michael, I want to go."

He saw the passion in her eyes.

"Take Alex, John."

"I don't need a physicist."

"But you do need another *voice*," Alex said.

He deliberated.

"Point taken, you can go. Bob, would you stay and monitor the frequency?"

"Sure, John, and I'll calibrate the LMI and radar, so we know how close it is, and how large."

"Thanks, Bob, anyone else have something to add?"

No one did.

Seven hours later, they still had not received a reply. The Mayday had stopped.

"It's time. Elan is the Shuttle ready to go?"

"Affirmative."

"Trent?"

"Wouldn't miss it, John."

"Alex tell Clifford and George to meet us by the Shuttle."

She made the call. They would be in their NASA suits.

"Change your mind, Alex?"

"To scientists, *all* matter—matters."

"Michael?" John asked.

He avoided eye contact with John.

In his logic tree, he didn't want Alex to go, but it was her decision, like Isaac told him. He knew the mission was dangerous. On the Russian ship, they would be vulnerable.

"I support Alex's decision."

"Then we better get moving. Bryan, we'll wear our helmet cams, so you can follow what's happening in real time. If for some reason we get jammed up, fire on the ship, understood?"

"Not until you're away in the Shuttle."

"No, if we encounter trouble and can't respond, you take out the ship!"

"Understood, John, I will order the strike."

"Stay focused, no emotional decisions, understood?"

They indicated agreement.

Alex, Elan, Trent, and John left for Launch Pad A where the Shuttle stood upright.

After they arrived, they put on their NASA suits, and verified the helmet cams were functional with Bob.

One by one they took a seat in the Shuttle.

Elan programmed the MFC to fly to the Russian ship.

"What about the hatch? Will it connect with the ship?" John asked.

"Yes, the hatch is the same on both the Shuttle and the ISS."

"Anyone need to go to the bathroom?"

Elan engaged the Shuttle's SE-15s. With all indicators green, he launched.

Along the ride, they stared out the windows looking for the ship. They saw a small light then the shape and size of the ship grew larger.

Elan monitored the Auto-Flight system as the Shuttle inched closer. Contact was made.

Elan shut down the thrusters.

They waited, but no one opened the Russian hatch.

George got out of his seat, opened the Shuttle hatch, and reached across the airlock for the external lever to open the ship's hatch.

There was no one in the Russian ship to meet them.

John took the lead.

Alex was the last out of the Shuttle.

It was dimly lit inside, their helmet lights helped until Elan and John found the light switch.

"Trent, your ghost ship theory has more empirical evidence," John said.

Their helmets had carbon scrubbers, so the stale air could be cleaned instead of carrying heavy oxygen bottles.

They followed a short corridor, which intersected with a main corridor.

Trent read the signage. The flight deck was to the right.

They proceeded with extreme caution, either the occupants concealed themselves, or Trent was correct.

They passed several airlocks and opened each. They didn't find much.

Clifford did a DOI.

They scanned for what John called "trip wires," anything that didn't look right, as they searched for the crew and colonists.

At the end of the corridor was a turn to the left, which took them into the flight deck.

"Трахать!" Trent said.

"What did you say?" John asked.

"It's a *f*expletive."

Annunciators flashed. Fans turned. All systems

were on automatic.

The flight deck was deserted.

"It must be a ghost ship, why leave it on Auto-Flight?" Elan asked.

"As soon as I wrap my head around it, I'll have an answer," John said.

"How's the air quality, Clifford?" Elan asked.

"I did a DOI, and didn't detect any. I can't speak for the air quality."

Elan undid his helmet until he smelled a horrifying, nightmarish odor. He shoved it back on fast.

"What, Elan?" John asked.

"The smell of death."

Their faces changed. Their fear rose.

"Let's go find the remains, and search for the ship's log."

"I'll search the computers since none of you can read Cyrillic," Trent said.

"I'll stay with Trent, so he can tell me what the instruments and switches are," Elan said.

"Alex, still think coming here to save them was a good idea?"

She broke eye contact.

"We'll start down the other corridor."

They moved together. No one wanted to search alone. They walked to the next airlock on the left. It opened.

They went inside and found what was left of the colonists and crew, four men, the rest were women, and children.

The bodies were stacked in piles on one side of the Food Station.

Baker examined the decomposed bodies.

"Bryan, are you seeing this?"

"Every step, John."

"I'd guess about seventy to eighty?" George asked.

"I count four crew uniforms," Alex said.

"Clifford, can you determine what they died of?" Bryan asked.

"I'll do my best."

"If there's viruses, or infectious diseases, get off the ship immediately," Bryan said.

John left the others. He walked across the corridor and opened the airlock. He entered the Cryo compartment.

There was one man in an operating cryo-bed.

One cryo-survivor? I'd hate to have his nightmares.

Clifford walked in to report his findings and was shocked to see the man.

"I see we have a survivor."

"Crazy, huh?"

"They died of a mystery infection, John. I won't know what it is until I get a sample back to the lab. None of them died an instant death because there was no frothing from the nostrils, or mouths."

"Bryan, there is a man in a cryo-bed. He's alive," John said.

Bryan called John back after they talked it over in ComCen.

"You *must* bring him here. We need to talk to him, to find out what happened."

"His cryo-bed won't fit into the Shuttle. Clifford will have to defrost him."

"I'm not certain I can, Bryan, everything is in Russian, and I'd be guessing on how to get him out, because I don't know how their system works. If I get him out, odds are he will die."

"Ask Elan and Trent to help."

"I will, Bryan, after they figure out how to engage the propulsion systems, and operate the ship," John said.

"No rush, our new friend isn't going anywhere."

"The ship is."

"We'll worry about the cryo later, unless Elan, or Trent, turns something off by mistake."

Alex walked in, sickened.

"Dad it's awful, they're women and children."

"Alex, get back into the Shuttle," Isaac said.

"No, Dad, they need me here. I'll be okay."

Elan walked into the Cryo compartment.

"What have we got here?"

"The answer, if we wake him. What did you and Trent find?" John asked.

"Trent showed me what turned on and off. He'll program the computers for Titan. We're going back to look for Propulsion, and see what's moving the ship."

"Take a look inside the compartment across the corridor," John said.

Elan walked to the compartment and saw the bodies.

He went back into Cryo.

"Gruesome, sad. Any idea what killed them, Clifford?" Elan asked.

"A contagious infectious disease. As they died, they stacked them in there. The last was a one-year-old child. Can you imagine what the child went through?"

"They were desperate, Alex was right about that. They left this gentleman behind for a reason. Can you figure out how to defrost him?" John asked.

"I don't know how it works. Maybe Trent can look at it," Clifford said.

"I'll get him in here to tell you what it says. I do know, we need to get him out of there, if for no other reason than to find out what happened."

"Bryan wants him brought back to base," John said.

"There's only two ways to do that, wake him here and take him in the Shuttle, or..."

"What are you thinking?" John asked.

"If we can manage it, we could take the ship to Titan, park it next to SEEDS-2025."

John looked at Elan while he contemplated flying the ship.

At best, it would prove to be a challenge.

At worst, they could, because of the language issue, crash into Base Crater.

"Let's think about it. Right now, we figure out how to get the survivor out of the cryo-bed. If we wake him here, and he checks out with the doctor, we can take him in the Shuttle," John said.

Trent heard the conversation in his helmet and walked to find them.

He walked into Cryo compartment and repeated

his *f*expletive.

"Трахать!"

"I sat on the flight deck with you for over a year and you never uttered one *f*expletive."

"Sorry, it seems to be the right word here. Who's this?"

"Don't know, but Bryan wants him back on Titan," Elan said.

"In or out of the delivery box?"

"I can't read the words to get him out," Clifford said.

Trent looked close at the cryo-bed, read the instructions. He told them how it open it.

"I told John once we figure out how to fly this thing we could take the ship to Titan and park it next to our ship," Elan said.

"That would be best. If we get him out and something goes wrong, we won't have the tools to revive him like we have back home," Clifford said.

"Tell me what you want me to do," Trent said.

"Bryan, I'm leaving the survivor in the cryo-bed. Elan and Trent are going to look at propulsion and see if we can fly the ship to Titan, and land inside Base Crater."

"Your call, Commander."

Elan and Trent hurried back to propulsion with George in tow who stopped along the way to check other compartments on the ship.

Less than an hour later, they returned to the Cryo compartment.

"We should be able to fly it back," Elan said.

"Are you certain?"

"Yeah, you need to go with us to the flight deck because you're doing the flying. George will assist."

Clifford remained in Cryo to monitor the cryo-bed's occupant.

He didn't touch anything.

He waited until Trent came back to the compartment.

The rest went to the flight deck.

Trent explained the layout of the instrumentation, and what the switches did.

The PFD indicators were visual clues even if John couldn't read the words. The numbers were the same.

George took the other pilot seat and studied what was in front of him

Elan sat by the engine start switches and thrust levers.

They got as familiar with the electronics as possible.

Trent searched for the ship's log.

Alex contemplated where they were and what they planned to do.

Titan's thick atmosphere would make landing the Russian ship difficult, if not impossible. It was the only other world with liquids on its surface like Earth. Liquid methane evaporated from the surface, and formed extremely thick clouds. Like Earth, the methane clouds would rain down filling the lakes and rivers on the ground composed of liquid hydrocarbons.

"How far out are they, Bob?" Bryan asked.

"They should be here in three and a half hours judging by their present speed, assuming they have the fuel."

Bob had not slept since the moment he was told about the first Russian Mayday. He became a pivotal figure in the entire operation.

After years of conflict with Bob, Michael changed his view of him as he watched him work."

"The time is good. It'll give John a chance to get used to the ship's characteristics," Isaac said.

"John, Bob, I built a program for the ship's computers to navigate over the crater."

"Transmit the data, Bob."

He pressed transmit and the data traveled at light speed through the black of space.

Trent received the data and loaded it into the onboard navigation system.

Annunciators confirmed the data installed was correct.

John verified the Auto-Flight system was engaged then turned to the others.

"We have a gruesome task to perform. George, Elan, and I will eject the cadavers overboard. Alex, I want you to monitor radio transmissions. Trent keep working to find the ship's log."

"You're dumping them into space? It's an example of what I said before. Where is our humanity," Alex asked.

"Alex, they're dead, have been for some time. It's better to give them a space burial rather than take the chance of spreading the infection on Titan," Isaac said.

"John—"

She saw in his eyes there was no stopping him and turned away. She sat by the radios.

"It's the right thing to do, Alex," Isaac said.

"It's wrong to treat them like trash."

"It's right to protect our people," Isaac said.

Elan, George, and John left to remove the dead. They entered the closed compartment and took each cadaver on rolling carts to the disposal unit.

With eight bodies left, an accident occurred.

John's suit was sliced open by a ragged edge in the disposal unit. His suit lost pressure.

Elan and George were still in the food compartment placing bodies on the carts.

John began to lose consciousness and slid down a wall. He rolled face down.

Six minutes passed before they found and revived him. They called Clifford and told him to come to the disposal unit fast.

He didn't know where it was. It took nine minutes to find them.

He evaluated John's condition. He found a long gash under the tear in his suit and tended to it. He saw the wound was infected.

The deadly infection.

He told the others to place John in quarantine because the infection was fast-moving and contagious.

"John—" Elan said.

"Do what he says."

They placed John on the rolling cart and found a compartment to isolate him.

Clifford followed.

Elan and George returned to continue the disposal of the remains, the last six.

"Stay away from that jagged edge," George said.

Elan placed the last Russian colonist into the disposal unit.

They watched through the portal as the one-year-old girl drifted into space.

Elan watched longer.

"Clifford, is John in danger of dying?" Bryan asked.

"I need to do more analysis. I don't have enough equipment here to determine if he is, but it's my prognosis."

"If you return the Shuttle can we put the equipment you need inside, or the medicine you need, and get it to the Russian ship in time to help John?"

"No."

"What if all of you return in the Shuttle and leave the ship?"

"Then you risk exposing us to the infection. I don't know if it's an airborne infection."

John heard the conversation in quarantine. His eyes closed.

Alex, and those in ComCen, were in disbelief.

"John, Isaac, you heard Clifford's prognosis. I want you to know we will do everything we can to find a way to save you."

John didn't reply. He knew his fate.

Silence traveled through space on the frequency. John spoke.

"Trent, have you programmed the Auto-Flight to Titan?"

"Yes, John, everything Bob sent. We can even auto-land. I found the log. It appears we should be more concerned with the *Chinese*."

His words hit as hard as hearing about John's condition.

Heads turned in ComCen.

Mind's raced at light speed.

"Elan?"

"Yes, John, I'm here."

"What is the condition of the thrusters?"

"They'll get us home."

"You did it in the simulator, and you've flown the Shuttle. It will be up to you to get the ship to Titan. Let the automation do the work. Make sure the MFC is reliable, and keep the guide bars on the PFD centered like we practiced. Try to get Brenda on the Shuttle when you get closer and have her go to the ship so she can assist. If she can't get to the ship, have her on the frequency to talk you through it. You can do it, Elan, I know you can. It's an order from the Commander of the ship."

"John, Clifford will find a way to get you stable."

Silence on the ship. Silence in the ComCen.

"Do me a favor, Elan, and tell Brenda I love her."

Alex walked up to the quarantined compartment and saw john lying on the table, Clifford standing next to him. She placed her hand on the view port.

"John?"

"You were right, Alex."

"I don't want to be right. I want you to live."

"I'm afraid, it's been decided. The good news is

when my body dies my energy will leave for the universe. I can find John, Sr., and my mom."

"John, you're not going to die. You can't! We need you, John. Brenda needs you. I need you."

"If only I could command it. Trent said it. 'To be, or not to be.' It's not to be, Alex. I'm grateful I was part of SEEDS. Grateful for Bryan and Isaac, you and Michael, everyone at SEEDS."

Alex looked through the view port at Clifford.

He indicated it was over for John.

"I love you, Commander John Kelly!"

"I love you too, Alex."

She couldn't watch him die. She put her back against the wall and closed her eyes.

"I'm headed to the flight deck, John, Trent wants to go over some things. You were always my best friend, ever since you rode in the AirTran with me. I'm sorry, John, I wish it was me," Elan said.

"No you don't, but you're correct, it's been a fun ride, Elan."

He left for the flight deck before someone saw his tears falling. He arrived on the flight deck and verified Trent's programming.

Clifford checked John's vitals.

"You heard what Bryan asked, about sending the Shuttle to Titan to get the equipment I need, or to take you in the Shuttle now."

"Clifford, you and I know it would be a useless endeavor, besides, all of you may need to evacuate this ship."

"Bryan, John, I want them all to return in the shuttle. They should wake up the survivor, and take him back in my seat. It makes more sense than to bring the Russian ship to infect the colony. Once they leave, I can get out of quarantine, and do what I can with the ship. Bob sent the programming. Trent loaded it. I can monitor. If I think the ship won't make it, I'll divert it away from Titan."

"It's a logical move, John," Bryan said.

"Are you absolutely certain, John, that's what you want?" Isaac asked.

"I want to spend the time I have left, in the command chair. Trent said, according to the ship's log, we should be more concerned about the Chinese. You must get the log and the survivor to Titan no matter what. I'm sending Clifford to defrost the Russian. I'll call after the Shuttle has gone."

Clifford heard everything, so did the others.

He examined the infection one last time. It was aggressive and spreading.

"Here, this is for the pain, John, it has been an honor to serve with you on board SEEDS-2025."

Clifford turned to leave.

"Thank you, Clifford, for taking care of my dad."

Clifford didn't look back.

He motioned for Alex to walk with him.

They joined the others on the flight deck.

George returned to the quarantine compartment.

"Thank you, John, for taking me along on the journey. I will never forget you."

"Take care of them, George, get them home safe."

"The door is unlocked now. Goodbye, John."

He walked back to the flight deck. They shared a hug. Clifford and Trent went to defrost the Russian.

"Looks like he's coming around," Trent said.

The man was dazed. Clifford examined him. Trent gave him water. The Russian couldn't believe he survived.

"Как ты себя чувствуешь?" Trent asked.

"I speak English. I feel light-headed and dehydrated. Who are you, and why are you on my ship? Where are my crew and passengers?"

Alex thought it would hurt less coming from her.

"I'm Dr. Alexandra Arthur. This is Dr. Clifford Baker, Dr. Elan Mason, Dr. Trent Garth, and George TwoBears. Dr. Baker and Dr. Trent revived you from stasis. The Commander of SEEDS-2025 is John Kelly. He was injured and is in quarantine with an aggressive infection. He will not survive much longer. We received your Mayday on Titan, and flew here to meet your ship because we did not receive a reply when we answered your distress call. I'm sorry to have to tell you this, but you are the only survivor."

He wept. His pulse elevated.

Clifford made him lie down.

After several minutes, his head cleared.

"I am Captain Boris Vladovok, commander of RED STAR 1. You are in grave danger."

"Why," Elan asked.

"The Chinese will come to your base, and do to you what they did to my people. They are all dead, only who you found, escaped. We sought your help with our women and children, and to fight the Chinese."

"Captain Vladovok, now that you have been revived, we must leave on our Shuttle to Titan," Elan said.

"I die with my ship and crew."

"I understand how you feel, but you are *not* going to die on your ship. Our Commander Kelly will be dying for you. We need you to return with us, so you can tell us about what happened on Mars. We will give you a chance to settle a score."

"Settle a score?"

"Do to the Chinese what they did to you, Sir."

They helped him into his flight suit and to the Shuttle.

"Bryan, we have a Captain Boris Vladovok returning with us to Titan. He has a lot to tell us about the Chinese. We are boarding the Shuttle now."

"Understood, Elan, come home."

Elan boarded first to show George how the Shuttle automation worked.

He went out to assist the others.

George studied the automation.

Alex entered next, followed by Vladovok, and Clifford.

Trent had a downloaded copy of the ship's log.

Elan made sure they were harnessed in.

To their surprise, he turned and exited the Shuttle locking the hatches of both ships behind him.

"Launch, George, Godspeed."

The Shuttle separated from the Russian ship, and

its automation orientated it toward Titan.

It accelerated until they could no longer see the Russian ship.

Elan went back to John who was surprised to see him.

He helped John stand, and to the flight deck.

"What are you doing?"

"I told you back on Titan, I wanted to fly the ship. I just didn't think it would be this one."

"Elan Mason, you are a crazy man."

"No Robonaut is going to deprive you of a flight. I'm making sure of it."

Elan helped strap John, and then himself, into the forward-facing captain, and co-pilot seats.

As soon as the Shuttle broke free from the Russian ship and was far enough away, Elan reprogrammed the MFC. He looked over at John.

"Maximum thrust!" John said.

Elan pushed the thrust levers full forward.

Both best friends flew the ship to the Milky Way.

Before the ship's fuel tank's were depleted, Elan watched John slump in his seat. He knew John was almost gone.

Elan closed his eyes.

When he opened them, a bright light appeared in the distance.

Elan struggled to look at it.

It approached the Russian ship precipitately.

Elan thought the ship was under attack. He didn't know where the defensive weapons were, or how to use them.

The light enveloped the ship.

Elan heard the bulkheads banging.

He thought he was hallucinating.

He heard something behind him, and turned.

Two figures walked to him.

They weren't human, but they held out a circular object to show Elan.

It was from Voyager, Carl Sagan's message to other lifeforms.

The two ethereal figures made a waving motion.

Elan watched John's body rise out of the captain seat and float away with one of them.

The other figure raised an appendage and signaled for Elan to follow.

Elan was led to their ship and followed the semitransparent figure inside.

John lay on a platform in an alcove. A brilliant light flashed over John.

Elan covered his eyes and turned away.

When the light faded, he saw John was resurrected.

The End

Thank you for reading
SEEDS The Journey Begins
If you enjoyed the story, please tell
your friends on Facebook, and Twitter,
and write a review.

About the author

"Cary Allen Stone is one superb writer!"

—Grady Harp, Amazon Hall of Fame Top 100

Reviewervine Voice

Cary Allen Stone spent forty years inside the cockpits of corporate jets and airlines. His flying career gave him a unique perspective on life. In 1992, he flew for Sir Ridley Scott, and when not searching for locations, Sir Scott mentored Cary on his writing. Cary graduated from college with a Bachelor of Arts degree. Author, filmmaker, voice-over, commercials, audiobook character voices, and standup comedy. He is an Amazon bestseller.

Find Cary Allen Stone at:

Website:

http://caryallenstone.com

Email:

caryallenstone1@gmail.com

Facebook Author page:

www.facebook.com/caryallenstoneauthor

Made in the USA
San Bernardino, CA
08 June 2019